Danger Patrol

Danger Patrol

Wayne D. Overholser

THORNDIKE
CHIVERS

This Large Print edition is published by Thorndike Press®,
Waterville, Maine USA and by BBC Audiobooks Ltd,
Bath, England.

Published in 2006 in the U.S. by arrangement with
Golden West Literary Agency.

Published in 2006 in the U.K. by arrangement with
Golden West Literary Agency.

U.S. Hardcover 0-7862-8326-2 (Western)
U.K. Hardcover 1-4056-3699-8 (Chivers Large Print)
U.K. Softcover 1-4056-3700-5 (Camden Large Print)

The text of this Large Print edition is unabridged.
Other aspects of the book may vary from the original edition.

Set in 16 pt. Plantin by Carleen Stearns.

Printed in the United States on permanent paper.

British Library Cataloguing-in-Publication Data available

Library of Congress Cataloging-in-Publication Data

Overholser, Wayne D., 1906–
    Danger patrol / by Wayne D. Overholser.
        p. cm. — (Thorndike Press large print Westerns)
    ISBN 0-7862-8326-2 (lg. print : hc : alk. paper)
    I. Title. II. Thorndike Press large print Western series.
PS3529.V33D36 2006
   813'.54—dc22
                                           2005030818

Danger Patrol

The First Day

Chapter I

My part in Turner County's trouble started the day I was twenty-one. My father and I were sawing up the winter's supply of wood in our backyard when we saw Judge Willoughby riding up our lane from the county road. My birthday was no holiday. Pa was never one to be idle for any minor reason. Nothing short of a death in the family would keep him from doing a day's work.

Not that I blamed him. The Logans had been on hard scrabble rations longer than I'd been alive. We had moved here from the San Luis Valley when I was three, so I didn't remember any home but the Rafter A, a ten-cow spread on the western side of Sunrise Valley, the poor side. All the good grass was east of the North Fork and had been gobbled up years ago by Pappy Jordan. His Anchor was the big spread of the county; everybody knew it and accepted it.

I tossed a stick of wood onto the pile as Pa wiped his face with his bandanna. It was only four o'clock and he didn't like to see the tag end of the afternoon wasted.

He stared at the judge for a full minute before he wadded up his bandanna and stuck it into the back pocket of his Levi's.

"What do you suppose the old bastard wants?" he grunted.

"We'd better go see," I said, and started around the house to the cottonwoods that shaded our front porch.

A visit from Judge Willoughby was the last thing I expected. It had never happened before and I doubted that it would ever happen again. I was curious about why he was here, but more than that, I was happy to stop work for a while. It was a hot day and I was tired. Besides, my twenty-first birthday was a big occasion to me, so I guess my nose was a little out of joint with Pa ignoring it the way he was.

The Judge reined up in the shadow of the cottonwood and nodded at Pa, who had come up behind me, then at me. "Howdy, Abner," he said. "Howdy, Ed."

We spoke, and Pa said, "Get down, Judge. Let's go try out the rockers on the front porch. I'll get Nancy to make us some lemonade."

The judge hesitated, staring thoughtfully at me, and then turned his gaze to Pa. He was an old man. He was also a big man with a white beard and mustache, and a quiet dignity that went with being a judge. He was one of the two most respected men in the county, Pappy Jordan being the other.

We should have been honored by the judge's visit, but we weren't — Pa because he resented the waste of time, and me because I was vaguely uneasy. I don't know why, but I'd often had feelings like that, a nagging hunch that told me something was going to happen that I wouldn't like. Later I was reminded of the line I had read so often in novels: If I had only known.

The judge cleared his throat and shook his head. "I've got to get back to town, Abner." He pinned his gaze on me. "I rode out here today to ask a favor of Ed. I don't want a quick no, son. Maybe you can't make a decision right off the bat, but I sure want you to say yes. The trouble is we can't wait very long for your answer."

Some of my hunch disappeared, and I was too curious to go on being uneasy. The idea of the judge asking a favor of me was too much to grasp. I said, a little impatiently I'm afraid, "What is it? I'll probably do it."

The Judge cleared his throat again, then he said, "I know you're young, Ed, but people respect you. I also know you're tough and strong, and you don't get rattled as easy as most. You've been raised to be honest and do a day's work. That's important." He hesitated as if expecting to be turned down. Then he blurted, "Oh hell, what we want is for you to serve out the rest of Bill York's term as sheriff."

For a moment I was too stunned to answer, or even think coherently. I just stared at the judge, then looked at Pa who was about as stunned as I was. I didn't answer. I couldn't.

Finally the judge said impatiently, "If you're worrying about the pay, it's one hundred dollars a month. Your term will last a little over a year and you might not get reelected, but you'd have a job for a while."

Finally I was able to say, "I didn't know York had quit. What happened?"

"Oh, I'm sorry," the judge said. "I forgot you wouldn't have heard. He was thrown from a horse a couple of days ago and broke his neck. As you know, we have no deputies or even a marshal in Purgatory. The sheriff is the only lawman we have in the whole county. It's been years since we had any real trouble, but we don't like to go very long without a lawman."

"I don't have any experience, Judge," I

said. "I'm too young. Folks will be calling me The Kid Sheriff."

The judge smiled and nodded. "You'll have to get used to that. All you'll have to do is to ask them if they want the job. Nobody wants it but Max Moran, and you know what he is. He'd be worse than nothing. That's one reason I rode out here today and the reason we need to know if you'll take it. We can ignore Moran for a while, but there is an immutable law that says nature abhors a vacuum. If we don't fill it with a man who can do the job, Moran will work up enough pressure on his side to get the appointment."

"Ed, if it's a matter of you or Moran," Pa said, "you'd better take it."

I was surprised Pa would say that, but then I knew Moran. He was a down-at-the-heels horse trader who had a little outfit on the far south end of Turner County. He was a known liar and cheat, with a reputation so bad that nobody who knew him would have any dealings with him. He was the kind of man who'd take the star and collect his pay and do absolutely nothing.

When I still hesitated, the judge said, "I met with the county commissioners this morning, and you were the unanimous choice. I promise that if there is any trouble, we'll give you all the backing we can."

"I dunno," I said, speaking very slowly and thinking that if the next year went the way the last ten had gone, downright peaceful and quiet, I could handle the job. "I'm helping Pa. I don't know who he'd get to help him."

"I'll make out," Pa said. "The Rafter A ain't so big that I can't do the work. I'll hire a man if I get in a pinch."

I knew then that he'd been thinking I wouldn't be here much longer. In the old days, Purgatory had been a boom mining camp, and Turner County had had a population of ten thousand people, mostly miners and honest townsmen along with the usual sprinkling of gamblers, pimps, whores and con men.

There had been plenty of jobs in those days, but now that the price of silver had dropped out of sight and the mines had pretty well played out, we didn't have five hundred people in the county. Cattle raising was about the only industry we had. Young men left the county as soon as they were grown, and the middle-aged men who had businesses had stayed and now were old.

I could see the judge's point. Turner County didn't have many men who were young enough and skookum enough to take on a lawman's job. I thought a moment about the salary. I could save most of what I'd make. I'd wind up with a nest egg so I could buy a business or a small spread, or do whatever I liked. There was a girl in Purgatory named Sharon Hall who would help me make the decision when the time came.

I guess it was that notion more than anything else that made up my mind for me. I said, "All right, I'll take it."

The judge smiled as he held a hand down to me. As we shook hands, he said, "Good, I knew you were an ambitious young man, so I had a hunch you'd take it. I want you to understand this is a commitment on your part to serve only the balance of the current term of office. If you decide you like the job and want it for another term, you can run on your record. If not, you can turn the star over to someone else."

What he was saying was plain enough. I was on trial. If I didn't work out, the commissioners could look around for someone else or even send for a man from outside the county. That was fine with me. A year might be all I'd want. From what little I knew of Sheriff York's duties, it had been mostly a matter of throwing drunks into jail on Saturday nights and turning them loose on Sunday morning. The job might turn out to be downright boring.

As the judge started to rein away, I said, "One thing. If something turns up that's more than I can handle, I want the authority to appoint a deputy and I want the county to have the money on tap to pay him."

"You'll get it," the judge said. "As I told you, we'll back you with everything in our power."

I was still curious about why they had singled me out and before he could ride away, I said, "I'm still not clear why you think I can handle it."

He laughed. "Well, you may think this is a pretty poor way to measure a man, but I've watched you play baseball. I've seen you take a throw when you were a catcher and stand your ground no matter who was sliding in to home plate or how big he was. I figure that if you wouldn't back up under those conditions, you'd stand your ground no matter what the problem was."

He touched up his horse and rode away. I stood staring at his back for a couple of minutes, wondering if this had really happened or if I was having a dream. Then I thought of what he said about me playing catcher, and I had a crazy impulse to laugh. I had been the catcher on the high school team and then the town team after I'd graduated, but it had never occurred to me that I was lining myself up to wear a star.

Then I thought again about the salary I'd get. I'd given it a lot of thought the last few months about what I'd do after I was twenty-one. I'd never hit on anything because I had less than one hundred dollars in the bank. I owned a saddle horse I called Alexander the Great, a buckskin I'd raised from a colt. I also owned a saddle, a .45, and the clothes on my back. What it boiled down to was that my future lay outside Turner County. There weren't any jobs for me around here.

Suddenly Pa's voice broke through my thoughts. "Come on down out of the clouds, son. Let's go finish the wood."

He walked away and I followed him around the house, the smoldering rebellion that had been in me bursting into flames. This would be the last time I'd do the work that he demanded of me. He couldn't say, even now, "Let's take the rest of the day off and go fishing."

There were times when I hated my father.

Chapter II

Neither of my parents had said anything about the day being my twenty-first birthday beyond a casual remark at breakfast, so I thought they planned more or less to ignore it. That surprised me because Ma always baked a cake, and she and Pa gave me something, even if it was no more than a new bandanna, so it seemed strange they would overlook this birthday, the most significant one of my life.

When I came in after doing the chores, I discovered I hadn't been ignored after all. Ma had fixed a good supper. She had killed a rooster and had made dumplings with biscuits, mashed potatoes, honey and pickled beets. She hadn't heard about my new job until I told her between bites. She didn't say anything, but seemed to freeze. For a long time she just sat staring at her plate as she ate.

Pa gave a short laugh. He said, "Ain't you proud of Ed, Ma? He'll earn one hundred dollars a month. I don't know what else he could do in this county to make that kind of money unless Pappy Jordan hired him to ramrod Anchor."

She looked up from her plate defiantly. "Of course I'm proud of him, but I don't cotton to the notion of him being sheriff. He's just . . . just too young."

"I figure I'll grow up pretty fast," I said. "I'll have to."

"It's too dangerous," she said. "You won't get any praise for what you do no matter what it is. You'll get kicks from one side or the other."

Why, nothing's happened in this county for years," Pa said. "We don't have no bad men. The bank ain't worth holding up. He'll arrest a few drunks, do some paperwork, and spend most of his time sawing wood to keep the jail warm next winter. The county commissioners are so damn tight they won't even hire a man with a rig to saw it up. They'll just hand you a buck saw and tell you to go at it."

I thought Pa was making it up, but later I found he was right. At the time I was too much concerned about Ma to give the wood a second thought. She bowed her head again and was dabbing at her eyes. I looked at Pa and then at her, and all of a sudden I realized I had been taking a lot of things about my parents for granted, that their hair had turned gray and that time and hard work had cut deep lines into their faces. They weren't much over fifty, but a lifetime of work had taken its toll and I simply hadn't realized it.

Then Pa's voice broke into my thoughts. He said, "It ain't the end of the world, Ma."

She wiped her eyes and looked at me, trying very hard to smile. "I know, Abner. And Ed, I know you'll make the best sheriff that Turner County ever had. I've realized for quite a while you'd be leaving us soon after your birthday, but I guess I hate to see the day come."

She got up and went into the pantry. Pa cleared his throat and poured more sugar into his cup of coffee and stirred it. By that time I was pretty well choked up. We weren't a demonstrative family, but I had never doubted that they loved me. I knew, too, that I loved them. I just hadn't given it much thought.

Ma came out of the pantry with a three-layer chocolate cake that had a lighted candle stuck into the middle. She sat it down in front of me and I reached up and patted her on the back. She leaned down and kissed me. She said, "Blow it out, son, as soon as you make a wish."

I told myself I wished I would do a good job as sheriff and blew the candle out.

Then Ma handed me a knife and I cut generous slices and passed one to Ma and one to Pa, and kept one for myself. After we finished the cake, Pa rose and went into the front room. He returned with the .30-.30 that had hung on the antler rack near the front door as long as I could remember.

Pa handed the rifle to me. He said, "We wanted to give you something special for your twenty-first birthday, but damn it we just didn't have the money. This will have to do. I know you'll need it because there's no guns in the sheriff's office. It's another case of the county being so damn cheap they can't even furnish the sheriff's office with one Winchester."

I took it, looked at it and shook my head. "I can't take it, Pa. You need it for deer hunting."

"I'll get along all right," Pa said. "You'll need it worse than I will. I've got the shotgun and my old Colt .45. If I decide to go after a buck this fall, I'll come to town and borrow it."

"That's a promise?"

He nodded. "It's a promise."

"Thank you," I said.

I couldn't say anything more. I just sat there stroking the stock of the rifle and knowing it was hard for Pa to give it up. I was glad to have the Winchester. I'd used it on deer hunts ever since I'd been big enough to fire it. I'd need it, all right, sooner or later, and I couldn't afford to buy one. I looked up and swallowed hard. God, he looked old and tired. Funny, I had lived with him all this time and had never noticed it before.

"Thank you," I said, and got up and left the room.

I walked across the barnyard and past the corrals and across a hay field to the North Fork, and knew that this was a special time for me. It was a damned sight harder to leave home than I had ever dreamed. I looked at the mesa on the east side of the river. The Anchor buildings were up there, big and sprawling, typical of a rich and powerful ranch. Pappy Jordan could look out over the whole valley from his front porch and see most of his range and the little outfits like ours that lay west of the North Fork.

I didn't know how many head of cattle Pappy owned but he had eight or ten men working for him. He was rich enough to take off for Arizona or California for a month during the coldest part of the winter, and he was important enough to sit in on all of the meetings that decided county business whether he held an office or not. It was fair to say that for as long as I could remember Pappy Jordan, Judge Willoughby, and the banker, Simon Ross, had run Turner County.

I had never heard of Pappy Jordan making trouble for anyone. He was a generous, law-abiding man. When it came time to drive a herd to the railroad at Gunnison, Jordan always let any of the rest of us who wanted to throw in the few head we had to sell. In exchange, he expected us to furnish three or four men to help with the drive. I had been on three of them and had learned to respect both Jordan and his foreman, Lars Larson.

Jordan knew as well as the rest of us in the valley that when an Anchor steer wandered across the North Fork onto our grass someone was likely to have fresh beef for supper, but he never said a word about it.

I wondered how I'd face a situation in which I had to knock heads with Pappy Jordan. Or the banker, Simon Ross. They would just be too big for me to cut down to size. All I could do was to hope that such a situation never developed. I returned to the house and went to bed. It had been a day.

Chapter III

After breakfast the next morning, Pa said, "I'll saddle Alexander up for you. You get packed and the next time I'm in town with the wagon, I'll fetch your trunk."

When I left, Ma kissed me and Pa shook hands. Then I stepped into the saddle and rode off, lifting a hand in a farewell gesture. Purgatory was less than five miles from our place, the road running along the west side of the North Fork. The valley was only five or six miles wide at any point with snow-capped peaks on both sides. Mountains blocked off the south and where several creeks ran together to form the North Fork. On the north more peaks seemed to form another barrier, but here the river had cut through the mountains. The gap was not much use to us, though, because the canyon was so narrow and the sides so steep that a road could not be built through it. The pioneers who had first settled in the valley had been forced to build the road over the mountains.

We were a self-sustaining community in most ways. We had to be because we were isolated through much of the winter when deep snow blocked the only road out of the valley. We were used to solving our problems and never looked to any outside source for help. I'd be solving these problems, I thought, or helping to, now that I was the law. The idea scared the hell out of me, but there was no turning back now.

At this time of morning there was little activity in Purgatory. Folks just didn't hurry to get at whatever had to be done. Main Street was short, no more than a block long, and half the buildings facing it were boarded up. Fire had destroyed part of the business block years ago, but a few frame buildings had been erected recently and two brick buildings survived from the boom days: the Turner County Bank owned by Simon Ross, and the Mercantile, Mark Vance the proprietor.

The court house was a two-story frame building set in the middle of a block directly east of the business district. It went back to the boom days, when no one thought enough of the center for law and order to erect a stone or brick building. It had survived the fires only because it was apart from the other buildings. The jail behind the courthouse was built of stone. I guess the old timers were more concerned about having a permanent jail than a courthouse that would last.

I reined up in front and tied. No one was in sight, and as I went in I wondered if I was too early for the judge. I climbed the stairs to his office, which was directly across the hall from the courtroom. I had been here a few times attending trials, but I had never been in the judge's office. I hesitated, not sure if I should knock, but decided I wouldn't, that his office was public. I opened the door and went in.

The judge was sitting behind his desk reading an enormous legal tome. I had looked at books of that nature, and, although I considered myself a good reader, I found that the words made no more sense to me than chicken tracks. I wondered how any man could get anything out of such a book.

The judge glanced up, saw who had come in and rose. He walked around the desk to me and held out his hand. "I'm glad to see you, Ed," he said. "I take it you're serious about pinning on the star or you wouldn't be here."

I was surprised and a little irritated to hear him say that. As I shook hands, I said, "I told you I'd be here."

"You did indeed," the judge said, "but I

thought there was a chance that after you talked it over with your folks, you might decide you didn't want the appointment. It may turn out to be a dangerous job, you know."

"That's what my mother said." I shook my head. "I guess I'll meet danger when it comes, but I don't know how I'll handle it."

"No man does until the time comes," the judge said, "but I'm not worried about that."

He swore me in, handed me a badge and said, "Put it on, Ed. Let's see how it looks."

After I'd pinned it on my shirt, he nodded approvingly. "Good. Now then, I think you know your duties, but I will suggest that most of your work will be right here in town. However, you have jurisdiction over the entire county and I think it would be a good idea for you to ride out and visit our ranch folks from time to time just to give them proof that we have a sheriff who's on the job."

He paused a moment, stroking his beard as if wondering how much else he should say, then he went on. "Just one more thing, Ed. Come to me if you have any questions as to where your authority ends and the lawbreaker's rights begin. Now let's go down and you can look your office and the jail over."

We went down the stairs together and out through the front door. Max Moran was standing in front of the courthouse, his legs spread, a hand on the butt of his gun. He must have seen me ride into town and had been waiting for the judge and me to come out.

"Willoughby, you stinking son of a bitch," Moran bawled, "I heard this kid had been appointed sheriff. I applied for the job and Simon Ross said I'd get it, but no, I'm forgotten and this kid who ain't dry behind the ears gets the star."

He started toward us, a big, menacing man, drunk and murderously angry. The judge said softly, "This is your first job, Ed. He's breaking the peace and threatening a duly elected official."

If I stood still, Moran would attack the judge. I knew that what I did in the next thirty seconds might very well decide my success or failure as the sheriff of Turner County.

The judge was standing a few feet behind me and to my right. I saw Moran move toward us; I saw his gun slowly being lifted from his holster, and for maybe a split second I stood frozen. Then I came unstuck. I took one quick step so that I stood in front of the judge as I said, "Give me your gun, Max."

Moran kept coming, apparently wanting to be close enough to the judge to be sure he would kill him when he pulled the trigger. I don't think he even knew I had moved in front of the judge. His eyes were glazed; his features were twisted into a mask that showed only black, unreasoning rage.

I took two long steps toward Moran and drew my gun. He was almost on me then, the hammer of his gun back, the revolver leveled. I knocked his gun barrel down with my left hand as he fired, the bullet kicking up dust at my feet. I swung my Colt down in a hard blow across the top of his head. He went down in an inert heap in front of me, his gun falling from slack fingers.

I picked his gun up and slipped it under my waistband, then holstered my own. Now that it was over, I was scared and started to shake, but I don't think the judge noticed it. His words came to me, breaking through the fog that surrounded me. "Put him on his horse and start him out of town."

I didn't say a word, but starting Max Moran out of town was the last thing I aimed to do. Besides, I didn't have any idea where his horse was and I had no intention of looking for him. I ignored the judge's order. Instead, I grabbed Moran by the shoulders and started dragging him around the courthouse.

The man was too big for me to carry, so I kept on dragging him across the front of the jail which served as the sheriff's office and into the big cell which made up the left, back side of the building. I lifted him and dumped him onto a thin, filthy mattress. I stepped back into the sheriff's office, found the ring of keys hanging from a peg on the wall, and locked the cell.

I hadn't realized the judge had followed me until I turned to replace the keys. Then I saw him standing in the doorway staring at me with a strange expression on his face. Wonderment, maybe, and certainly surprise, but I didn't think I saw any annoyance because I hadn't taken his advice. Right then I decided not to apologize to him or explain why I had done what I had. I figured I was sheriff and I would fail or succeed by my own decisions.

The smell of the place was nauseating. It was hard to pinpoint what the smell was, but I suppose it was a combination of stale sweat, vomit and urine, all building up over the years. I had never been jailed, but I had been here a few times, and I had always wondered how old man York could stand it.

"I'm going to scrub this place out," I said. "There's no sense in it smelling like this. I want you to twist the commissioners' arms until they authorize me to buy some new mattresses. I'm going to burn these. Also I want to buy at least three Winchesters and several boxes of shells and lock them up in the gun cabinet." I nodded toward it. "Maybe I'll never need a posse, but if I do, I don't intend to waste an hour while they go home to pick up their rifles."

Maybe I was being overbearing and pushing my good will, but at the moment I didn't give a damn. A lot of things needed changing in this office and I was either going to get the changes I wanted or the judge could take his star back.

He nodded, a little dazed, I think, by my demands, but I thought I detected some respect in his expression. He had been treating me with the condescension a grandfather might give a grandson who was in the process of becoming a man.

"Go ahead and get anything you want that's within reason," the judge said. "Send the bill to Simon Ross at the bank. If the commissioners won't authorize payment, I'll pay the bills out of my own pocket."

He started to turn away, then swung back. "Oh, one more thing, Ed. You'll have to live in town and we can't have you sleeping in the mow of the livery stable. You can get a room in the hotel, but that will run pretty high. I own that little house just north of the courthouse. You can have it for five dollars a month if you want it. It's vacant so you can move right in. You can cook your meals, or take some at the hotel. I'll get Beulah Heston to give you a discount." He took a long breath, then said, a little grudgingly I thought, "You'll do, Ed."

This time he turned and left the jail. I started a fire in the stove and found a cord or more of wood piled back of the jail, all of it in four-foot lengths. I sawed up enough to heat the water, getting a little hot from my temper as I sawed. Finding a rig to saw up the wood pile was another change I was going to make.

I scrubbed the office, then the cells, but I saw it was going to take time and more scrubbing before I got rid of the smell. Moran was beginning to groan and stir when I finished. I left the jail, thinking I'd find some kind of disinfectant, which couldn't smell as bad as the stink the jail had, but before I stopped at the store, I decided to turn a block north and look at the house the judge was renting me.

I left Alexander in the shed back of the house, then went in. The judge had been right. Everything I needed was here: a bed in the tiny bedroom and plenty of covers, a kitchen with a range and dishes and pots and pans, and a front room furnished with an ancient leather-covered couch, a rocking chair, and a small, claw-footed stand in the center of the room. Several rag rugs covered most of the floor.

I could get Ma to give me a runner for the stand. I'd bring a few books from home and, after I laid in a supply of groceries, I'd be in business. I'd decide later how many meals I'd take at the hotel. I knew I'd eat some there because eating alone three times a day wasn't my idea of living. Besides, I was one hell of a lousy cook.

I swung around by Sharon's house before I went to the Mercantile. She was my age; we'd gone through school together and I guess we'd been in love back when we were kids still. We talked some about marriage, we both wanted it, and we knew that we couldn't do anything about it until I had a job that would support us, so up to now it had been only a dream.

Sharon lived with her mother, who had a dressmaking and millinery business, the only one in town, so she made a living. Sharon was about as skillful as her mother with both hats and dresses and, from what I could gather, did as much of the work as Mrs. Hall did.

I knocked on the door and a moment later Sharon opened it. She gave a shriek of delight and threw her arms around me and kissed me. I don't know how long we stood there, hugging and kissing and letting the other know how much we were in love, with neither of us giving a thought to time. At moments like this, I was carried away by a flood of desire that was almost more than I could handle and I think Sharon was in about the same predicament.

We were brought back to the material world when Mrs. Hall yelled, "Bring him in, Sharon. I like him, too."

Sharon drew back and patted my face. "What brings you to town in the middle of the week? Couldn't your father find anything for you to do?"

"I didn't ask him," I said. "I've got news for you."

"Come in and tell Mom, too," Sharon said and, taking my hand, led me into the room where her mother was working on a dress.

It would have been the front room of any other house, but for Sharon and her mother it was a workroom filled with a sewing machine, cutting table, odds and ends of vari-colored bolts of cloth and a counter covered with hats for sale. When Mrs. Hall saw me, she jumped up and hugged and kissed me, then patted me on the back. Sometimes I thought she loved me about as much as Sharon did.

I always marveled at the relationship between Sharon and her mother. It was nothing like my relationship with my parents, but more like that of two sisters. Mrs. Hall was in her late thirties, I guess, but she looked younger. They resembled each other. Both had blond hair and blue eyes, with slender figures and smiles that always made me feel welcome no matter when I dropped in.

"What's that about news?" Mrs. Hall asked. Then she noticed the star on my shirt and squealed, "Ed Logan, what have you been up to?"

"I'm the new sheriff of Turner County," I said. "I just took the oath."

They stared at me for a long moment, neither appearing to breathe, then Sharon dropped into a chair and began to cry. Mrs. Hall said, "That's real fine, Ed."

I told them about Judge Willoughby's visit. I didn't look at Sharon, who sat with her head bowed and kept wiping her eyes. Women, I thought disgustedly. She was as bad as my mother.

"You'll make a fine sheriff, Ed," Mrs. Hall said. "Now then, Sharon, just what is the matter with you?"

"I don't want him to be sheriff," Sharon wailed. "Somebody will kill him."

"Oh, I don't think so," her mother said mildly. "Nothing has happened like that in this town for a long time. Now if it had been in the mining days . . ."

"Mom, you never know," Sharon cried. She swallowed and made another dab at her eyes. "Somebody could hold the bank up and Ed would have to go after him."

"No, that won't happen," I said. "There's not much in Simon Ross' bank for anyone to get if they did, so nobody'll try."

Sharon didn't say another word, but just sat with her back against the chair as stiff as if she were frozen there. She kept wadding up her handkerchief in her lap, then she'd straighten it out and wad it up again. Her mother chewed her lower lip as if she couldn't figure out what had bit Sharon. I felt the same way. As long as I had known Sharon she had never cried except once when she was hurt and that had been years ago.

"You can bawl your head off," Mrs. Hall said finally, "but I think it's wonderful that Judge Willoughby thought enough of Ed to ask him to serve as sheriff. That means your judgment in young men is excellent."

Sharon relaxed and unexpectedly giggled. "I guess that's right, Mom." She rose and came to me and kissed me. "I'm proud of you, Ed. It's just that I don't know how I'll be as a sheriff's wife."

"I've been thinking about that," I said. "Maybe you'd better start practicing. I'll be making enough money for us to live on. The judge is letting me have that little house he owns back of the courthouse for five dollars a month. It's not big, but it would do for us."

She jumped up. "I'll think about it. Now I'm going to put dinner on the table. We've got chicken soup and Mom cooked a cherry pie this morning."

She ran into the kitchen. Mrs. Hall sighed. "I want you two to be happy, Ed. If you'd ask me to marry you, I'd say let's do it tomorrow, but Sharon's not ready for marriage. She's just been playing with the idea. I know you're made for each other, but you'll have to wait. You're both young. Please don't rush her."

I nodded, thinking glumly that she was right, but couldn't help wondering when a girl became a woman.

Chapter IV

The banker, Simon Ross, was a genuine, twenty-four-carat son of a bitch. I guess a lot of bankers have that reputation. Most of the time it wasn't deserved, but it was with Ross. Pa had asked for a small loan twice and had been turned down. There seemed to be no reason for it, because he was a better risk than some of the small ranchers and farmers who were granted loans.

The only reason we could figure out for Ross turning Pa down was the simple fact that Pa was not an ass-sucker. Sometimes he was brusque of manner and he refused to call any man Mister. Simon Ross liked to be called Mister. I think he viewed himself as the king of Turner County, and I guess any man who controls the credit of a county can just about be considered king.

Ross was a county commissioner, along with two farmers who lived below town. Being the kind of man he was, possessing both money and power, he controlled the vote of the other two commissioners. I still couldn't account for the fact that the three of them had agreed on me for sheriff, but I think Judge Willoughby put it to them that I was available and nobody else except Max Moran was. The judge and Pappy Jordan were the only two men in the county who could influence Ross. Maybe Jordan had recommended me.

When I left Sharon's house, my stomach filled with chicken soup, pie and two glasses of milk, I decided I might as well call on Ross. I'd have to sooner or later. I wasn't stubborn as Pa. I could call a man Mister. But I didn't intend to grovel. I wasn't sure I could find any in-between ground to stand on, but I had to try.

When I went into the bank and told the teller, Alec Simpson, that I wanted to see Ross, he motioned me on back to the banker's office. The door was open, so I went in. Ross was sitting at his desk, very busy with a legal looking document.

He knew I was there and was standing across the desk from him but he ignored me. It was his way to ignore a visitor for a minute or so. This procedure established the proper relationship between banker and customer, but I wasn't a customer at that moment and Ross wasn't a banker, and I was damned if I was going to stand there until he decided to notice me.

"I'm serving as sheriff, Mr. Ross," I

40

said. "I came in to notify you that I am making some purchases for the office and the judge told me to send the bills to you and the commissioners will pay them."

He laid the paper on his desk and looked up, frowning. I suppose because he was irritated that I had not waited for his sign of recognition.

"Logan," Ross said after a moment in which he gave me a cold stare, "there are some things I want to make clear to you at the start. I want you to understand that you are a temporary appointment. By giving you the star for a few months, we will have time to find someone who will fill the bill adequately."

He might as well have thrown a bucket of cold water on me. In essence that was exactly what he was trying to do. I'd never had much to do with him, but I'd had enough to know that I thoroughly despised the man and that he considered me nothing more than an ant to squash under the sole of one of his patent-leather shoes.

He was a small man, quite bald, with a thin, weasel-like face and pale blue eyes that might have been chipped out of ice. Now he had taken pains to cut me down to the size of an ant. It was all I could do to keep from shaking him until his teeth rattled.

I stepped forward to the desk and leaned across it. I said, "Ross, I don't really care why I was appointed. The fact is I am the sheriff and whether I serve more than the balance of this term will be up to the voters of Turner County, if I decide to run. Now if you don't want to know about what I'm going to . . ."

He held up a hand. "Oh, I want to know, all right, but you'd better learn right now that the commissioners will not accept any bill you send us. You will pay it yourself if you buy anything without our authorization."

"Oh, you'll pay for whatever I buy," I said. "Not me. The judge told me that he would pay it out of his own pocket if you commissioners refused payment. If that happens, I will see that you get plenty of publicity regarding your decision and what the judge had to do." I started to leave, then paused. "One thought just occurred to me. God help you if for any reason you have to appear in Judge Willoughby's court after he has paid bills the county should have paid."

I stalked out of Ross's office, thinking to hell with him. I might have known an interview with him would turn out this way. He yelled, "Now wait just a God-damned minute, Logan, . . ." but I kept on across the lobby of the bank and out into the warm, fall sunshine.

I didn't know how much damage I had done to myself, but I thought I had handled the banker the only way I could, that if I didn't make my position clear now, I never would. I was sure I had been picked because the commissioners thought I could be told what to do, as young as I was. They were dead wrong, and the sooner they found it out, the better.

My next stop was the Mercantile where I bought three .30-.30s, several boxes of shells and a bottle of disinfectant. Mark Vance, the storekeeper, acted as if he was uncertain about whether he should sell me the guns, and when I told him to send the bill to Simon Ross for the county to pay, he started shaking his head.

"I can't do that, Ed," he said. "You have to get an authorization from the commissioners so I will know they have agreed to pay the —"

"They haven't agreed to pay, Mark," I said, "but they will."

I picked up my purchases and headed for the door. Vance yelled, "Damn it, Ed, you can't take those guns until you see Mr. Ross and get . . ."

I was in the street by that time and I didn't look back. I went on to the jail in long strides. If anyone had passed me on the street, he would have considered me a complete idiot the way I was grinning. I felt good. I had power and I had used it. And for just a few seconds I knew how Simon Ross felt sitting behind his desk and deciding the financial future of the men who came into the bank, hats in hand, to ask for credit.

The stink in the jail was almost as bad as it had been before I'd scrubbed the place. I opened the gun cabinet, placed the rifles inside, set the boxes of shells beside them and locked the cabinet. Moran had come to, and when he saw me he got up from the cot and rattled the bars with one hand, holding his head with the other as if he was afraid it would split wide open.

"Let me out of here, damn it," he bellowed. "You haven't got no grounds to hold me on."

"Attempted murder is plenty of grounds," I said.

"How long?"

"How about till next summer?"

He started to curse me, then stopped when I said, "You're not helping yourself a bit. I intended to release you tonight, but

44

now I'm not going to."

He stopped, staring at me as if he couldn't believe what was happening. "You ain't dry behind the ears, sonny," he said slowly. "You can't make folks believe you're the sheriff. What do you think is going to happen to you?"

"I'll have some trouble," I admitted. "Fact is, I've got trouble already. I just told Simon Ross where to go. A man can't have much more trouble than that."

He took a long breath. "I don't believe it. Nobody tells Simon Ross nothing. You're a fool if you try to." I started toward the door to get some wood so I could get a fire started when he said, "I'm hungry, Logan. You fixing to starve me to death?"

I hesitated, not realizing until he'd called my attention to it that part of my job was to see that the prisoners were fed. "I'll get you some grub as soon as I start a fire," I said.

Ten minutes later I walked into the lobby of the hotel. When I didn't see anyone, I went on through the dining room into the kitchen. Beulah Heston was sitting at a table with her hired girl. They were peeling potatoes and didn't hear me come in until I was halfway across the kitchen.

When Beulah saw me, she jumped up,

half a dozen potatoes dropping from her lap and rolling across the floor. "Why, if it ain't the new sheriff," she screamed and grabbed me around the waist and hugged me.

To the good women of Purgatory, and this included my mother, who ordinarily was not one to gossip, Beulah was the town whore. She may or may not have been. All I knew was that she kept a hotel that had clean rooms and put good meals on the table in her dining room. It was her business if she slept with some of the drummers who stayed overnight at the hotel when they were in Purgatory. It wasn't my business to criticize her morals, and it still wasn't, now that I was the law.

"The judge told me you had been appointed," Beulah said, "and that you might be taking some of your meals here. He told me to give you a discount on them."

I hesitated, looking down at her. She was young middle age, maybe forty, with a few gray hairs and lines in her face. She was a little too plump and a little too eager with too much makeup on her face. I wasn't sure what was in her mind, but she sure as hell had an expression of expectancy on her face.

"That would be fine, Beulah," I said.

"How does fifty percent sound?" she asked.

That about knocked me over because I thought ten percent would be generous. I said, "Fine, but isn't that more than you can afford?"

"Of course I can afford it," she said testily. "It's like the judge said. You're not going to get rich wearing that star and you're going to be risking your neck. We owe you something, Ed."

"Thanks," I said. "I'll be taking some of my meals here. I'm not sure how many."

"Any time you want to come," she said. "You can pay at the end of the month. I'll give you a bill figuring the discount. And another thing. The judge said he was going to offer you that little house he owns, but I thought you might like to stay here in the hotel. I've got a good room in the back of the hotel. It's quiet and I think you'd like —"

The hired girl started to snicker. She wasn't very bright, and I guess the work she did for Beulah was about all she was capable of doing. She broke in, "Beulah figures a young buck like you would be good in bed."

Beulah whirled and slapped her across the face. "Keep a decent tongue in your

47

head, Annie," she said, and turned back to me, her face red. "You've got to overlook what she says, Ed. She don't know nothing."

The girl looked abashed, tipped her head down so she couldn't see me and kept on peeling potatoes. I said, "I've got a prisoner who says he's hungry. I guess you've always furnished grub for the prisoners."

"Oh, I sure have," she said. "I'll fix a meal right away and take it over to him."

"Good," I said. "I've heard that jail food has been pretty lousy. Let's start giving the prisoners something decent to eat."

"We sure will," she said heartily.

I left the hotel, knowing damned well that there had been some filthy talk about me between Beulah and Annie, or Annie wouldn't have said what she did. I felt uneasy about my relationship with Beulah. I couldn't help doing business with her, but I had a nagging hunch that the damned girl was going to make up some fancy lies about me.

I knew one thing for sure. Beulah Heston was never going to get me in bed with her.

Chapter V

I scrubbed the jail and office again, this time using the disinfectant, and when I'd finished, I decided I had improved the smell, although I wasn't sure the odor was much of an improvement over the original stink.

Beulah brought Moran's meal to the jail just as I wound up the scrubbing. I took the tray from her and carried it back into the jail, noticing that the roast beef, potatoes and gravy, biscuits, coffee and pie looked as good as anything I'd ever had in Beulah's dining room. I grinned as I thought how Simon Ross would scream when he got her bill.

I had been thinking about my conversation with Ross. It bothered me a hell of a lot more than I had thought it would at the time. The truth was I had to prove myself. The only way I could do it was by handling some sort of violent crime, something that hadn't happened in Turner County for years. Ross would do all he could to force me to quit, perhaps even asking for my resignation which he wasn't going to get.

It wasn't just that he was a proud and powerful man. He was genuinely mean, and I knew he would never forgive me for what I had said, but he had no hold on my parents or me. The question was how much pressure I could stand. Certainly I had to have cooperation from some of the county people.

For instance, if I needed a posse, I'd have to find men who would serve. Most folks didn't like Ross, but they were afraid of him, and I had a terrible feeling that fear was a stronger force than a sense of responsibility to the law. Even more than an emergency, the daily relationship with the people of the county would decide whether I held the job. I could stand Ross' hatred, but I couldn't stand it if people simply turned their heads and refused to speak when we met on the street.

There was one thing I could do and that was to see Ernie Faust who published the *Purgatory Weekly Press.* He was an old friend of Pa's who came out to the ranch every fall and went hunting with him. He had always liked me, and I knew he would give me a fair shake in his newspaper.

As soon as Beulah left, I headed for Faust's print shop. He was standing at a table cutting paper when I went in. He glanced up, saw who it was, and turned from the table.

"Howdy, Ed," he said affably. "How do you like being sheriff? I see you've got your star polished up all bright and shiny."

"It came that way," I said. "As to how I like the job, I'll have to wait a few days before I know. Right now I've got a problem."

He looked at me questioningly, then jerked his head toward the back of the shop where he kept a pot of coffee on the stove. It was always warm. He drank a gallon of the stuff each day, and he always visited with his callers over a cup of the brew, which was strong enough to take the lining off a man's throat. I had trouble swallowing it, but I didn't want to offend him, so I followed him to the back of the long room and sat down while he poured coffee into two mugs and handed one to me.

"I guess you can call me a father confessor to half the people of Turner County," he said. "Now if you want my advice, I'll give it to you free, and that's exactly what it's worth."

Ernie Faust was an institution in Purgatory. He was one of the early settlers, bringing a Washington hand press across the mountain from the San Luis Valley the year the silver strike was made on the North Fork. He had seen the boom and the decline of business in the county, but he had stayed on, not making much money, but earning a fair living because he never spent much.

He seemed to be very old, although I don't think he was in years. His face was deeply lined, most of his hair was gone, and he walked with the slow gait of a man who was uncertain whether his next step would keep him upright or send him sprawling. He was honest beyond question. He had often displayed rare courage on controversial questions, and he was respected in a strangely affectionate way. I say affectionate because other prominent men like Judge Willoughby and Pappy Jordan were respected, but most people's feeling ended with respect. I did know he had never bumped heads with Simon Ross, but then no one else had, either, except me.

I hesitated as I stared down at the tarlike contents of my mug, then I jumped in with both feet, telling him about the judge's visit and adding that I was surprised by being appointed. I wondered how much, if any, Pappy Jordan had to do with it.

"You can bet on one thing," Faust said. "He was consulted. If he had anything against you, or if he had any reason to think you couldn't handle the job, he'd have squashed your appointment."

"That's what I thought," I said.

I told him about my set-to with Moran. He nodded. "That's a story I can print, which I will in telling about your appointment. It will do you some good. I think you came in here because you know damned well that folks will be critical of your appointment. They'll say you're just a kid who's too young to carry the star. This story will make them think a couple of times before they voice any criticism."

"I thought it would," I said, "but there's something else."

I told him about my run-in with Ross and he shook his head, sipping his coffee and staring at the wall across the room. "Ah, the temerity of youth," he murmured. "Handling Moran was one thing, but taking on Simon Ross is something else."

He got up and walked around the table, then sat down again, still holding his mug. "Of course that's one story I can't print. I'd say, if you will permit an old man's criticism, that you didn't use prime judgment the way you talked to him. He'll never forgive you because he's a very petty man. I would say his dignity is as important to him as his profits."

"I know that," I admitted, "and you're right, I should've kept my mouth shut, but it seemed to me that if I didn't make a show of being my own man, I'd be in trouble the rest of my term. Right now I'm not thinking of running again. I just want to be allowed to do my job the way I see it."

"Aye." He nodded. "I savvy that, but you see, when you deal with a man like Simon Ross, you swallow your pride and you try to be as diplomatic as your temper will permit because you know that, if you are going to do your job in this county, you've got to get along with the man. How far you go in swallowing your pride is another matter."

He rose and set his mug down on the back of the stove. He picked up the pot and immediately put it down as if telling himself he had drunk enough of the awful stuff for awhile.

He turned to face me. "I've been down this road a good many times. He's got me whipsawed because he can close me out any day I go to the bank asking for my note to be renewed. I don't like to talk about it, but I've done more than my share of pride swallowing. It always seemed like I didn't have any choice. I'm too old to move to another town and start over. It's different with you. You can say to hell with it and ride off to wherever you want to go."

I'd felt uneasy ever since I'd left the bank. I knew I hadn't handled Ross well, that I'd been so determined to be my own man that I had gone out of my way to alienate the banker. My father was a stubborn man, and I had often resented that stubbornness just as I had yesterday when he had been so set on finishing the woodcutting on my birthday. I had never realized before how much I was like him and I wasn't happy with the thought.

I picked up my mug and took a drink of the black stuff and almost choked. I set the mug down. "I know you're right, Ernie, about swallowing my pride. I should have, I guess, but can't go back and apologize, so I guess what I'm really wondering is how hard he can make it on me."

"He'll try to make it hard," Faust said, "but if you keep your nose clean, I don't think he can do you much harm. On the other hand, if you make some horrendous mistake he'll have you. He'll remind folks that he said something like that would happen. How many people will be convinced that he was right is the question."

He took his pipe out of his pocket and filled it, smiling. "I've been here a long time, Ed, long enough to know what I'm talking about. I've always said that living in Purgatory is the same as living halfway between heaven and hell, and most of the time you're going to be closer to hell than heaven."

I had occasion to remember that remark many times the next few days. I walked along Main Street to the Mercantile, thinking I had lived in the county most of my life and I had always got along with people. Now, the very first day I was in office I crack Max Moran on the head and jail him, then I go out of my way to make Ross sore at me. Mark Vance, too, I thought bleakly, but I knew I'd act the same way if I had to do it over again.

When I gave Vance my order, he said, "If this is another bill to go to the county, you get to hell out of here right now."

I laid a ten-dollar gold piece on the counter. "It isn't," I said.

He started putting my groceries on the counter, eyeing me sourly every time he turned toward the counter to lay something down. Finally he said truculently,

"By God, Ed, if the county won't pay for them guns, I'll take it out of your hide. I can't afford to lose that much money."

My temper began roaring up in me just as it had in the bank, but this time I was determined to keep a lid on. I leaned across the counter until my face was about two feet from his. I said slowly, "Mark, any time you want to take something out of my hide, you're welcome to try."

He backed up as fast as if a hornet was chasing him. "All right, all right," he said. "I just hope to hell the county pays the bill. That's all."

I took the groceries home, home being the judge's little house, and I smiled wryly at the thought of this place being home. I couldn't believe what had happened to me in the last twenty-four hours. I had been telling myself for months that I'd leave my parents home after my twenty-first birthday, but I hadn't given much thought about where I'd go or what I'd do.

All I knew was ranching and there were mighty few ranch jobs in Turner County. That meant I'd have to leave the county, and winter was coming on. It was no time of year to be caught without a place to live.

Sure, I could ride the grub line. A lot of cowboys did, but that wasn't my idea of a way to live, not with Sharon Hall waiting for me. But then, and the thought was a sour one, maybe Sharon wasn't really waiting for me. That was something I had to find out.

I didn't have enough groceries for supper. It was going to take some time and thought to stock my pantry so when I finished putting away the items I'd bought, I headed for the hotel. The stage came in late in the afternoon, and I knew old man York always met it.

York liked to say he met the stage just as a matter of principle jokingly adding that if a gunslinger showed up in town, he wanted to know about it. Seriously I considered it a good principle. Not many strangers came to town except drummers, and few of these were strangers, so if somebody showed up who wasn't what he seemed to be, I'd probably spot him, but whether I'd be able to figure out who he was was something else.

As usual, half a dozen men were standing in front of the hotel, most of them old men because this had become an old man's town. Not that they had any real reason for waiting for the stage. It was cheap entertainment for them, about the most exciting thing that happened in Purgatory, but usually they were disappointed.

More times than not the stage rolled in empty.

I knew all the men, and as soon as I joined them, they yelled various greetings such as "How's the new sheriff?" "Hey Ed, where'd you find that tin star?"

It was all good-natured joshing and I recognized it for what it was. There was none of the hostility I had found in Moran and Ross and I felt better. What happened to my career as a lawman would depend on what I did, and I'd been plagued ever since I'd left the bank that I'd have folks against me on the grounds that anyone my age couldn't do the sheriff's job.

The preacher, Caleb Watts, came up just after I got there. He held out his hand, saying, "I was glad to hear you were appointed sheriff, Ed. You'd have been my choice if the board of commissioners had asked me."

He smiled as we shook hands, and suddenly the day took on new brightness. He was a young man, older than me, but not by much. I had always liked him, even though I did not go to church as often as my folks thought I should.

I said, "Thanks, Caleb. That means a lot to me."

And it did.

Chapter VI

Somebody yelled, "There he comes." A moment later the stage roared down Main Street straight toward us and stopped in front of the hotel, a cloud of dust boiling up around it. The driver, old Abe Negley, had been driving the stage for years and he always made the most of his big moment.

"Got any purty passengers aboard, Abe?" a man yelled.

Negley didn't answer until he stepped down, then he said with pride, "You're damned right I have," and opened the door with a flourish.

A woman stepped down and the crowd became silent. She was young, dusty and tired, but nobody would deny that she was pretty. She turned toward us briefly, smiled, then swung back to face the stage while Negley dug her bag out of the boot.

"I'll carry it into the hotel for you, ma'am," he said, and picking up the bag, strode past me into the hotel.

She followed, reaching me, and, glancing in my direction, saw the star on my shirt. She stopped, her gaze moving up to my face. She asked, "Are you the town marshal?"

"No, ma'am," I said. "I'm the county sheriff."

She hesitated, her expression thoughtful, her gaze pinned on my face, then she asked, "Are you as young as you look?"

"I'm afraid I am," I said.

Someone in the crowd yelled, "Younger, ma'am."

Everybody laughed and she smiled. "I'm Caroline Dallas," and held out a slender, gloved hand. "I must see you. Will you give me fifteen minutes to wash up, then come to my room?"

I hesitated, thinking this was a very strange request coming from a young, pretty woman who had just stepped down from the stagecoach, then I took her hand and said, "Yes ma'am, I'll be there."

She smiled again, said, "I'll expect you," and walked past me into the lobby.

Several men whistled and one of them said, "Just like wearing a uniform, Ed. Women can't resist a star."

"By God," another man said, "purty women never invited me up to their rooms. How do you do it, Ed?"

I ignored them. I hadn't noticed until then that a man had also stepped out of the coach and was waiting for his bag. He grinned as he looked at me. He said, "You're a lucky man, Sheriff."

I knew he didn't mean anything, but I still resented the remark. I nodded and mumbled, "I reckon."

He was in his middle forties, I guessed, a solid, good-looking man dressed in a brown broadcloth suit with a gold chain across his vest. He was wearing a black derby hat. He was a businessman of some sort, I thought, although I couldn't guess the business.

His face was a dark tan, so he'd spent much of his time out of doors. There was something else about him, too, that I couldn't quite put my finger on, a sort of competence, a sense of self-confidence that said he could handle anything that came his way. He would be, I thought, a man to reckon with.

Negley handed his valise to him and the man took it, then set it down and held out his hand. "I'm Charlie Lambert," he said. "I hope you won't think I'm parroting the young lady, but I also want to talk to you. However, I'm not in as much of a hurry as she was. Later this evening or tomorrow morning."

I nodded, my curiosity stirring. "My

name's Ed Logan. I'll be here."

"Good," he said, and, picking up his bag, went on into the hotel.

"I'll be damned," somebody said. "Ed, you're the most popular man in town, now that you're sheriff."

"Looks like it," I said.

The crowd scattered, but Caleb Watts remained. He said hesitantly, "I don't often stick my nose into your business, Ed, but this strikes me as being mighty odd, two strangers getting off the stage the first day you're in office and both wanting to see you."

The first thought that came to me was to tell Caleb he was indeed sticking his nose into my business, but I didn't, knowing that I was becoming unduly proddy and he was one of the best friends I had.

"I know," I said. "What do you make of it?"

"I sure don't know," he answered. "Maybe there's no connection, but on the face of it, I'd guess they're in cahoots and setting up some kind of a scheme. I'm not a man of the world and neither are you, so it's a little hard for us to savvy a situation like this." He scratched the back of his neck, frowning. "It occurs to me they might be planning to blackmail you for some nefarious reason. Satan appears in many ways wearing many masks, and a woman's pretty face is one."

"She's not getting me into bed with her if that's what's worrying you."

"It isn't so much evil," he said, "as the appearance of evil that will hurt you. Well, I hope you'll forgive me, but I had a hunch about this I felt I should mention. And Ed, if there is anything I can do for you, let me know. It's to all of our interest that you succeed. I have been very much aware that York was not adequate for the job and I know you are. It's just that people have to be convinced."

He turned and walked away. I knew I should not resent what he'd said. I knew he was dead right, and I was convinced his offer to help was genuine. Still, I was disturbed with his statement about Satan. I guess that was what had cooled me off about going to church. It seemed to me that preachers and church people in general were more interested in condemning evil than they were in praising good. Still, his warning was sound and I knew very well that I was being plunged into what might become quicksand. I could be over my head before I knew it.

I stepped into the bar and had a drink,

waited for what I guessed was fifteen minutes, then walked to the desk, turned the register and found the number of Caroline Dallas's room. When I climbed the stairs, I found that her room was one of two that looked out over Main Street and I was curious why the clerk had given it to her. These two were considered choice rooms and were better furnished than the others, so they cost one dollar more for a night. Money, it seemed, was not as important to her as it was to most people who put up at the Purgatory Hotel.

She opened the door to my knock and said, "Come in." I stepped inside, a little uncertainly because I couldn't forget the preacher's warning. She motioned me to a chair. "I apologize for speaking about your age. It's just that I expected a sheriff to be an older man with a black, drooping mustache."

She laughed as she sat down on the bed and faced me. I liked her, warning or not. She just didn't strike me as being Satan's tool. I had a better chance to size her up as we sat in silence for a moment looking at each other.

She was about twenty-five, tall and slender, with auburn hair and blue eyes. I don't know that everyone would have called her pretty, but she had an openness and directness about her that I had seldom felt in women, a trait I admired. Pretty or not depended on each person's sense of beauty, but she was attractive beyond any question.

"Well," she said, "You're going to hate me because I'm going to drop a load of trouble into your lap. You don't know it, but hell is going to break out in this county, and it's possible that if you're warned you can do something about it."

She paused, her head down, her gaze on her hands that were folded on her lap. Then she looked up and blurted, "You know that Pappy Jordan had sold Anchor?"

"No." My heart stopped beating, then began to thump. "He couldn't," I said hoarsely. "He's an institution. He can't leave. It's the same as if you'd told me the North Fork had started to flow uphill."

"Then the North Fork is flowing uphill," she said. "It's the reason I'm here. The man who bought it is my brother-in-law. His name is Dan Kramer. He had owned a big outfit east of Trinidad. I should say my sister owned it, but she doesn't count. He does everything and she accepts it. They will be here tomorrow, I think."

I hadn't seen Pappy for several weeks

and I hadn't heard he even intended to sell. I just couldn't grasp the fact that he had. For me it was impossible to think of Turner County with Pappy Jordan gone, but he must plan on leaving if he'd sold. There'd be no reason for him to stay.

"You'd better tell me the rest of it," I said. "I don't savvy why this man Kramer and your sister getting here will cause all this trouble."

"You will when I tell you about Dan," she said sharply. "I hate him. I want him dead. I'll kill him myself, or maybe you will, but he's got to die. He's a fiend, Sheriff. He's diabolical. I hate to think what will happen to your county if he's not killed."

Suddenly her face, which a moment before had been a pretty one, pleasant and friendly, became so contorted by the hate that flooded through her that she was transformed into a vindictive monster. I had never heard so much venom in a person's voice. She began to tremble, the corners of her mouth worked and tears rolled down her cheeks. She stopped and clenched her fists, then wiped her eyes with a lace-edged handkerchief.

"I don't let myself go that way very often," she said in a low tone. "I used to.

After he raped me. Now I'm able to handle it most of the time because I don't talk about it, but you've got to know. You see, my younger sister is not very attractive, but she was my parents' favorite because she was easy to handle when she was growing up and I wasn't. Now I'm older, I can look back and see I was a brat.

"Dan started with us as a top hand when I was a teenager and Sis was ten. He's a good cattleman, and when our ramrod was killed in Trinidad in a gun fracas, Pa hired him to run the outfit. Rheumatism bunged Pa up so bad he couldn't ride and he left everything to Dan. I knew Dan was a bastard from the first because he made advances to me that were indecent but neither of my parents would believe anything bad about him. So I finally quit telling them.

"He married Sis when she was sixteen. She was so fat the boys never paid any attention to her, so I guess that when Dan proposed, she thought she'd better get a man when she could, although maybe she did love him then. Who's to know?"

She rose and walked to the window. She stood with her back to me, dabbing at her eyes and struggling with her feelings. After a time she turned and started talking again.

"I went away to college. Denver University. I graduated and got a job teaching in Denver. I didn't go home because I was afraid of Dan and because I quarreled with my parents so much. Finally they disinherited me and left everything to Sis, which meant to Dan because she always accepted any decision he made. She just couldn't stand up against him.

"My father died in his sleep last summer, or so they say. I believe Dan murdered him, but I don't have any way to prove it. I have to admit I hate him so much I would naturally think that. I know Pa had been in poor health for a long time. Anyhow, I went home for the funeral. While I was home, Mamma died, which was understandable because she'd always lived for Pa. When he was gone, she simply didn't want to live.

"The night before I left, Dan came into my bedroom after I had gone to bed. He said he'd wanted me from the day he came to work for us and now he was going to have me. I started to yell, but he hit me across the side of my face and said he'd kill me if I didn't submit. I still fought him, but he's a strong man and he succeeded. The next morning, he was gone. I tried to tell Sis, but she wouldn't listen. She said I had always hated him and was making it up just to turn her against him. I left later that morning, but before I did, she admitted they had not been getting along.

"We've been writing. He abused her after our folks died and now she's afraid of him. That's why she wrote me about his plans. She didn't want to sell the ranch. I guess they had a terrible fight, but in the end he beat her down. I think she believes now he did rape me. Anyhow, a few days ago she wrote that Dan had sold the place for a big figure and had bought Anchor. He has some kind of a deal brewing that will make him a fortune. I don't know exactly what it is, but it is big or he wouldn't be into it. That has always been his goal, to make a million dollars."

She returned to her chair. "That's the story. I know very well that you don't believe all of it, thinking that I hate the man so much that I'm not telling it straight, but when he gets here, you'll find out. He intends to buy the small outfits west of the river so his holdings will include the whole valley."

I rose. I knew he couldn't do that. Too many of the small owners, my father included, liked their homes too well to sell and Kramer couldn't afford to give them as much as it would take to persuade them to sell.

"I guess we'll have to learn to live with him no matter how big a bastard he is," I said.

"No, you won't be able to live with him," she said. "You're going to have more trouble than you ever dreamed about because he'll kill the men who won't sell."

Chapter VII

When I left Caroline Dallas's room, I felt as if I had been hit by a bolt of lightning. Someday Dan Kramer would kill her sister, she'd said. When his plans were worked out and he had his million dollars, he'd find a way to get rid of his wife. She just wasn't the kind of woman a man like Kramer wanted to finish his life with.

It was the last thing she said just as I was leaving her room that set me on edge. He was bringing in a known killer named Buck Sharkey who would persuade the little ranchers to sell out. I'd heard of Sharkey. Most people in the West had. I guess he was as much legend as man. I don't suppose he had committed all the murders that were laid to his door, but he was beyond doubt ruthless and efficient, and he was known to have committed enough murders to demand and receive a high figure for his services.

According to the stories I'd heard, he would kill a man from ambush or face-to-face, whichever the situation called for. This meant he was fast on the draw, which most dry gulchers were not, and that made him doubly dangerous. I'd also heard that no one knew for sure what he looked like, that several men who had killed in the manner he did simply disappeared after they'd earned their money. No one seemed to be sure which one was the real Sharkey.

I crossed the lobby and for a moment stood in the doorway staring into the street, deserted except for a couple of Plymouth Rock hens scratching in the dust in front of the livery stable and a big, brown dog sleeping peacefully in the middle of the street. I had been aware from the moment I had pinned on the star that I was under the gun, that I had to handle any situation that came up if I was going to prove to the people of Turner County that I was capable of doing the job, but I had never in my wildest nightmares expected to have to face a man like Buck Sharkey.

Even more important was the fact that I had to prove to myself I could rise to the occasion. If I lost my confidence, I couldn't cut the mustard. For a sickening moment I knew damned well I couldn't face Sharkey in a street fight and outdraw him. If I had to do it, I'd die, and I sure as hell didn't want to die tomorrow. I was willing to die when it was time, maybe fifty years from now, but not tomorrow or the day after tomorrow. Not at least until I had slept with Sharon Hall and fathered a child.

Some people believe that is the way a man becomes immortal. I knew only one thing for sure. Now that I have pinned on the star, I couldn't run. It just wasn't in me. That was one thing Pa had dinned into me from the time I could walk. Don't ever run from anything, he'd said over and over.

Pa hadn't. I knew that for a fact. He'd never been a great success by some standards, but he'd worked hard and he'd made a living, and he'd always stood his ground on anything that was a principle to him. The times when Simon Ross turned him down for loans simply made him go home and keep on working.

I stepped onto the boardwalk, thinking I had to see Sharon. Not that I was going to tell her what I was up against. I just wanted to pin her down on whether she'd marry me or not. She sure hadn't answered my question that morning. If she wouldn't, well, there were other fish in the sea. I wanted to talk to Caleb Watts. I'd do that on my way back to the jail. I had to look in on Max Moran.

Two steps were all that I took. It was

supper time and Sharon and her mother would insist on putting another plate on the table. I sure didn't feel like eating anything. The only thing I could do was to eat in the hotel, then I could tell them I'd had supper. It would be my business if I didn't eat much there, but that was never the case in the Hall home.

Just as I wheeled to go back into the hotel, Simon Ross left the bank. He looked directly at me and I looked at him. He didn't speak and I didn't speak. His face looked as black as a thundercloud about to burst into a raging storm. For a moment I thought he was going to come up to me and demand my resignation. He didn't, and I thought, irrelevantly, that he stayed late in the bank every day to avoid going home to Elvira. I didn't blame him for that.

When I stepped back into the hotel lobby and turned toward the dining room, Charlie Lambert came up to me. I guess he had been sitting in a chair in the lobby and had been watching me, but I had been so buried in my thoughts and fears that I hadn't noticed him.

"I'll buy your supper tonight, Logan," he said. "I've been waiting to see you. I've got some questions to ask before tomorrow morning."

"Sure," I said, and wished I felt like eating a foot-long steak if he was footing the bill.

"Good," he said as we walked into the dining room and took a table near the windows. "Anything I can do for you? You look like a man who's been staring at the face of death."

He was a hell of a perceptive man, I thought. "No," I said. "I just don't feel very well. I'll just have a bowl of soup and a cup of coffee."

"Suit yourself." Shrugging, Lambert picked up a menu and studied it, and when Beulah Heston came to the table to get our order, he said, "Big, thick steak, rare, a slab of apple pie, and coffee. Can you do it?"

"Of course, I can do it," she said. "What about you, Ed?"

"A cup of coffee and a bowl of soup," I said.

"Well, you're sure off your feed," she said.

I didn't say anything. She stood there a moment, her eyes on Lambert's face as if speculating about their future relationship, then she returned to the kitchen, her hips swinging in a seductive walk that made Lambert shake his head.

"That's a God-damned lecherous woman," he said, his gaze following her until she disappeared through the swinging door that led into the kitchen.

"She has that reputation," I said.

"You don't know her personally?"

I shook my head. "My mamma taught me different."

He laughed approvingly. "You've got a smart mamma." He settled back, took his pipe and tobacco can from his pocket, and dribbled tobacco into the blackened bowl. "I'll be candid with you, Logan, and I'd appreciate it if you didn't spread around what I'm going to tell you. It would make me a pile of trouble if you do."

I nodded. "I understand."

"You see, I'm a professional treasure hunter. I know that sounds crazy because most of the stories about lost treasure are myths, but some are legitimate. We know that there has been a lot of money lost in various ways and in various places in the West, most of it buried by outlaws who planned to come back, but didn't because they died, or went to the pen, or for some reason or another."

I nodded absently as Beulah brought our coffee, lingered a moment looking at Lambert again, her eyes hungry as hell. He shivered. After she'd gone, he said, "That woman gives me the shakes, Logan. She's the kind who'd wake you up in the middle of the night crawling into bed with you."

"She won't do that," I said. "She'll let you make the first move."

He struck a match, touched the flame to the tobacco and drew on the pipe, then sent a cloud of fragrant smoke into the air. "Well, that's a relief. I always hate to turn a woman down."

I was curious about his treasure hunting, so I asked, "Do you ever find any treasure that's worth the effort?"

"Oh, hell yes," he said. "I've done most of my hunting in Arizona and California, but there are some good prospects here in Colorado. This one in Turner County is about the best. The trouble with these old maps, if they are accurate — which they usually aren't — is that they were made years ago. Until you get into this business you don't realize how much the face of the earth changes over the years.

"You see, they always put down landmarks to guide them back to where they hid the money, but the landmarks change. If it's a tree or a snag or a deadfall, you can depend on it that it won't be there when you look for it. If it's a certain rock or a

78

landslide or a turn in the river, it may be different by the time you get there. Rocks move, landslides get covered by grass and brush so they don't look like landslides, and rivers change their course."

Our meals came. My soup was good, and I discovered that I was hungrier than I had thought. Lambert's steak kept him busy for a while, but when he finished he started talking again.

"What you have to do sometimes if the landmarks don't hold up is to try to figure out how it used to be. For instance, a tree might become a deadfall, so you have to guess where it grew if you can't see the stump or a depression where the roots might have been. It's a hell of a fascinating hobby. With me it's as much hobby as business. I've been successful and I've laid aside enough money to live on the rest of my life."

He leaned back and patted his stomach. "She's a good cook even if she lives a life of sin. Well, what I wanted to talk to you about was to get some advice about the county. I'll buy a Winchester early tomorrow morning, then rent a horse and start out. I want to know about people. Am I likely to run into some tough hands and have my horse stolen? I know it's supposed to be a peaceful county, but that doesn't mean there aren't any hard cases around."

"I don't think you'll have any trouble," I said.

"What about the wildlife? Bears? Mountain lions?"

"You might see some," I answered, "but if you let them alone, I'd say the chances are they'll let you alone."

"Grizzlies are the ones that make the trouble," he said.

"Nobody's seen a grizzly around here for years," I said.

Beulah came to our table and asked if we wanted dessert. I said I'd have a piece of apple pie. I considered what Lambert had said about a good treasure prospect in Turner County. There were a number of stories I'd heard Pa and Ernie Faust tell, but I'd always put them down as legends. Still, it must have taken more than a legend to bring a professional treasure hunter here, so I asked him.

"The stage from Gunnison was held up," he said. "It wasn't long after the mines were built. They were bringing the payroll in and they were behind a couple of months, so it was a big one. Three road agents stopped the stage north of town and took the strongbox, but it was empty when the sheriff found it hours later.

"The outlaws headed north to fool the posse, then swung back, kept to the river for a while, and intended to leave the valley by crossing the mountains to the south. They didn't know the county well enough and couldn't make it because the snow was too deep. They turned back and the posse nailed them about three miles south of town. They didn't have any of the money on them, so the sheriff figured they'd buried it before the posse caught them."

"You know where they left it?" I asked.

"Yeah, I know," he said, "but it's the same old problem. That's been a good many years ago, so it'll be a puzzle to figure it out."

"How'd you get onto it?"

"I know a fellow who spent most of his life in the pen at Canon City," he answered. "He shared the cell with one of the outlaws who held the stage up. Before he died in prison, he gave my friend a map. I guess he knew he wasn't going to live long enough to get out and look for the treasure and the other two had already died. My friend had intended for years to come here and hunt for the money, but he never could finance the trip. He's in poor health now and he knows he'll never do it, so he sold me the map."

Lambert rose. "Take your time with your coffee. I'm going to take a turn around the block. I'll pay for our suppers as I leave. I'm going to bed in a few minutes. Being jostled in that damn stage all day wore me down to a nubbin."

After he left, I picked up my cup of coffee, thinking about Sharon and wanting to put off calling on her. I guess I was scared she'd say no and with Buck Sharkey heading my way, I didn't need a turndown from Sharon.

I thought Lambert had gone for his turn around the block, but when I looked up, he was standing there looking down at me, a questioning look on his face. I guess he'd gone into the lobby and had come back.

"I'm a nosy fellow," he said hesitantly, "and you'd be justified in telling me to stay out of your business, but I'm going to say something. You can take it or leave it.

"When you ride all day in a coach with a good-looking woman like Caroline Dallas, you get to gabbing. She talked a lot about herself and her family problems, which were none of my business, but that's beside the point. I had heard of her folks and her brother-in-law, enough to know she was lying as fast as she could talk. I decided to warn you in case she gets you involved in her reason for being here, whatever that is. She never said."

Lambert wheeled and strode away. I finished my coffee, not sure what to think. Caroline Dallas had impressed me and I found it hard to think she had been lying, as emotional as she had been about it. On the other hand, Lambert had no reason to lie to me. He also didn't have any reason to tell me any of it unless he wanted to play father to a young and inexperienced sheriff.

I left the hotel and walked along Main Street toward Sharon's house. The air was beginning to cool now that the sun was down. In another hour or so it would turn downright cold. That's the way it is in the high country in the fall during the warm spell, hot in the sun and cold enough to be uncomfortable as soon as the sun drops over the line of peaks to the west. We'd had some cold weather earlier in the fall with a foot or more of snow in the mountains, then it had turned to Indian summer as it often did. The quaking aspen and scrub oak had turned so that both sides of the valley were slices of gold and fiery red.

My thoughts didn't linger long on the weather and mountain beauty. They turned back to Charlie Lambert, a jovial, friendly man I had instinctively felt was both confident and someone to be reckoned with. As I walked up the path to Sharon's house, all I could do was to hope to hell he was right, that Caroline had lied for reasons of her own, and that Buck Sharkey was a thousand miles from here.

Chapter VIII

Sharon opened the door to my knock and threw herself into my arms the instant she saw who it was. "It's Ed, Mamma," she screamed. "He's back again."

"Bring him in," her mother called.

Sharon was hugging and kissing me, and I would have thought it was great at any other time, but now I had words on my mind, not caresses. As soon as my mouth was free, I said, "Not this time. I want to talk. Get a wrap and we'll go for a walk."

She pulled her face back from mine, gave me a long, searching look as if wondering why I wanted to walk when I could stay there and enjoy our lovemaking. Finally she nodded and turned back into the hall. As she took a coat off the hall rack, she called to her mother, "We won't be gone long."

I stepped back and she came out, closing the door behind her. She put an arm around me and I slipped mine around her. We started walking. A lot of thoughts poured through my mind in the next few seconds, all of them shadowed by a grim one. What was I doing here, talking about getting married when I might be dead in twenty-four hours? I thrust the notion away and I plunged ahead.

"I've never told you I love you," I said, "but I'm telling you now. I guess I've been in love with you since we were in grade school. I knew we didn't have any chance of marrying, so I never said it in words. All this time I'm sure you knew I loved you even if I didn't say it."

"Of course I knew," she said, "and you knew I loved you. We didn't have to say it in words."

"That's the way I felt," I said. "I haven't asked you to marry me for the same reason. You knew that was what I wanted when we were able to do it. We are now, so I'm asking you. Will you marry me?"

She stopped. We had reached the corner and were standing in front of Simon Ross' house. I wondered if he was looking at us. Not that I cared, and I didn't care when she pulled my face down to hers and gave me a long passionate kiss. As a matter of fact, I hoped he was. He'd look at Elvira and be envious as hell.

A moment later she let me go. She said softly, "Of course I'll marry you, honey. I guess I would kill myself if I had to face my whole life without you."

We resumed our walk. I said, "That's not exactly what I wanted to hear. Your mother told me not to hurry you. I'm not trying to do that, but now that I've got a job with enough money coming in each month to support us, I thought we could set a date. I know the judge's house is small, but we can make out for a few months until something else turns up. It's only a couple of blocks from your mother's place. There's even plenty of furniture to make us comfortable until we save enough to buy more."

She didn't say anything for another block. We were out into the country then and walking along a dusty road. Finally she said in a funny, choked tone, "Ed, I don't want to set a date and then have to break it. I know what Mom meant. To me marriage has always been what I wanted, but never a definite date. It was just something in the future to look forward to, something that was going to happen but wasn't on the calendar like a birthday or Christmas. More like having a baby or taking a trip or something like that. Or even dying. A vague time. Can you understand that, Ed?"

"Yes," I said, "only that's not the way I

feel. I guess I want it so much that I've got to know when it will be so I can look forward to it. I've never had any money to spend. I like to play poker and have a drink or two on Saturday night. I'm afraid I'll blow it."

"No you won't, honey," she said. "Please give me a little time to think about it. I guess I'm a little afraid."

I stopped and turned her so she faced me. "What are you afraid of, Sharon?"

She tipped her head back so she could look at me. She said slowly, "I don't know. I mean, I can't tell you."

"Did your parents have a happy marriage?"

"Very happy." She swallowed. "I hope we can have one as happy, but I want you to live longer than Pa did."

I had a pang of conscience then. I hadn't told her about Buck Sharkey and I wasn't going to, but I knew that was the one thing that was pushing me. I had some kind of crazy notion that if I knew just when Sharon and I were getting married, I'd have the self-confidence to handle an impossible task that faced me, even to outdrawing Sharkey. When I thought of the possibility — no, probability — that I would live a hell of a lot shorter time than her father did, I felt a dull ache creeping all over my body.

But I had gone this far. I wasn't going to pull back now. I asked, "Did your mother ever talk to you about being married?"

"No."

I hadn't realized until that second that I knew more about what married couples did when they went to bed than Sharon did. Maybe a man always does. We had never talked about it, never even discussed how many children we would have or what we would do to keep from having the flock of kids that some couples do and thereby force themselves into a life of poverty.

"Please talk to your mother," I said. "Or come out and talk to mine, but I promise you one thing, Sharon. I will never force or abuse you, and I will be very gentle with you."

"Oh, honey, I know you will," she whispered. "That has never been my worry."

We turned and walked back to her house. She was crying softly. I felt damned guilty, as if I had already abused her. We didn't say another word all the way back to the house. When we reached her front door, she kissed me and said, "I promise I will talk to Mom. I'll have a date for you the next time I see you."

She stepped into the house and closed the door very softly. I walked away, not sure I had done the right thing, but I didn't regret what I had said. It would have had to have been said sooner or later; she had to be forced into facing married life if we were ever going to have one. As I walked toward the church, I felt a rising anger at Sharon's mother, who had not assumed a mother's responsibility.

The sun had been down for several minutes and the dusk light was deepening all over the valley. Now it was so thin that it was impossible to know for sure what was real and what was imaginary. It was, I thought, an ideal time for a killer like Buck Sharkey to dry gulch a man he wanted to murder.

I didn't think Sharkey was in town, and I wasn't even sure I was the man he was coming to Purgatory to kill. Still, the possibility that I was the man he wanted to dry gulch was frightening. I knew he would kill me if we faced each other in broad daylight on the street, but for some reason I wasn't worried about that. I was, on the other hand, panicky about being smoked down from a hiding place so I didn't have a chance to fight for my life.

The church was a community one,

leaning toward the Methodists. It was set close to the street, its tall spire reaching so far toward the sky that when I was a child I thought it must touch God in His heaven. The parsonage was a small, white cottage set behind the church. It would have been too small for a large family, but Caleb Watts and his wife had been here for three years and had no children. It was generally believed they would never have any unless they adopted some.

I walked around the church to the parsonage and knocked. Mrs. Watts opened the door and peered at me. When she saw who it was, she cried, "Come in, Ed. I'm so glad to see you. Caleb was telling me at supper about your appointment. Congratulations."

I stepped into the house and said, "Thank you."

She was a plump, good-natured woman who could sing, play the piano and get along with the diverse personalities among the women, some of whom were nit-picking old meddlers who seemed to have an undue influence in the affairs of the church. I liked her very much, and I knew that she and Sharon often sang duets for the church service and were good friends. She was probably the one Sharon should talk to about married life instead of her mother. I wished I had thought to suggest her. I had a strong conviction that she and Caleb had a lusty relationship.

Mrs. Watts closed the door and called, "Caleb, Ed's here to see you."

The preacher opened the door of his study and stepped into the front room. "Come in, Ed. I'm guessing you have some news."

"Some of it's good news," I said. "Sharon and I are engaged."

"Well now, that is good news." He extended his hand and I shook it. He called, "Florence, did you hear that? Ed and Sharon are engaged."

She ran out of the kitchen, smiling broadly. "It's about time, young man. I've been hoping to hear that." She hugged me and then stood beaming at me. "I'm so glad. I'll see Sharon in the morning and I'll . . ."

"Let her tell you first," I said. "She hasn't set a date and I think she wants to before she makes it public. I just felt like telling you and Caleb."

"I'm glad you did." She looked at me, still beaming. "I'll be close-mouthed, though it will be hard."

"Come on in, Ed," Caleb said. "I've got

a bad feeling that not all the news is good."

"No, it isn't," I said as I followed him into his study. "But then I'm not sure how much of what I learned since I saw you is really news."

I told him about my talk with Caroline. He leaned back in his swivel chair, hands folded across his stomach, and listened attentively. When I finished, he stared past me for a couple of minutes before he said anything.

"That's a lot of news," Caleb said finally. "I hadn't heard that Pappy Jordan planned to sell out, although I've known him for a long time. His wife is very bad with rheumatism and she wanted to leave the ranch. But about this man Sharkey? You really believe he's coming?"

"I'm afraid it's true," I said. "But then, I don't know how much she's lying, or even if any of it's true."

"I'm guessing she didn't tell you all there is to tell," Caleb said. "For instance, you don't know how much responsibility he had for the raping, assuming it did happen. In some cases, women invite it. However, from what she said, I can understand how much she would hate this fellow Kramer, even to coming here to get revenge."

"That's not all," I said. I told him about having supper with Charlie Lambert.

He laughed dryly when I finished. "Now that puts some frosting on the cake. You know I told you there was some connection between them. It was just a hunch. No real reason to think that. We don't get many strangers in town, but I suppose it's possible for two people to arrive on the same stage without having anything to do with each other. Now after you've told me what both of them have said, I don't have the slightest glimmer as to what the connection is."

I rose. I said, "I'll just have to wait it out and see what develops tomorrow. One thing I am going to do in the morning is to see Bud Campbell. I made the judge promise I could have a deputy when I needed one. Bud's my best friend. I guess he's about the only help I can count on in a pinch, but then I'm not sure I'll need a deputy, or what a deputy could do to help if I have a showdown with Sharkey."

He rose and came around the desk and laid a hand on my shoulder. "Bud may be your best friend, but he's not your only one. If you need any more help, you can count on me. I can shoot and ride a horse. I've never been tested, but when it comes to whether I live or die, with my courage on trial, I'll try."

"Thanks, Caleb," I said. "I think you'll be surprised if it comes to a testing. I've got a hunch we'll both be tested before this is over. I made an enemy out of Simon Ross this morning. I'm glad to know I have at least two friends."

"You've got more than that," he said. "I think you'll be surprised if it comes to a testing. As far as Simon Ross is concerned, he's the most pathetic human being I have ever seen. I doubt that he has a friend in the county."

"Not even Elvira?"

He grinned. "Not even Elvira."

I left, feeling better than when I'd come. They were good people, both Caleb and his wife, and his offer to help made me feel good. Not that I expected to call on him. It was just the idea that he had offered.

I stepped into the jail and lit a lamp. I held it close to the bars and looked at Moran who was sleeping on the cot, his snores a discordant sound in the night silence. I stood there a moment looking at him and wondering if there was any connection between him and the things that seemed to be happening. I decided not. That was reaching too far.

Then another question occurred to me. What would old man York have done if he hadn't died? I had no way of knowing, but if what Caroline Dallas had told me was true, nobody in Turner County was prepared to face what was coming.

I felt a chill run down my back when I remembered Caroline saying that Sharkey was being brought in to make sure that Dan Kramer's offers were accepted. What did that mean? Intimidation? Pa and Bud Campbell's grandpa and the others were stubborn men. They liked their homes and I knew damned well they'd turn Kramer down. What would happen then? Sharkey would kill some of them, then most of the rest would panic, sell out to Kramer, and bust the breeze getting out of the county.

I blew out the lamp and left the jail. I went to my new home, lit a lamp and looked around the little house. I went from room to room thinking it wasn't home. It would be until I brought Sharon here as my bride.

I didn't have any horse feed in the shed, so I rode Alexander to the livery stable. I returned to the house and went to bed, but not to sleep.

The Second Day

Chapter IX

I got up at daybreak, built a fire and made a pot of coffee. I still didn't have enough food in the house to fix a meal, so I shaved, drank my coffee and left the house. The air was chilly. The bite of fall was in the air. Snow was falling in the high country, and the peaks on both sides of the valley were a glistening white, so our Indian summer was about over.

I started toward the hotel to get breakfast, then thought about Moran and decided to turn him loose. I wanted to get him off my hands and not worry about him. After I had unlocked his cell and told him to go, I turned to hang the keys up and saw that he still stood in the middle of his cell.

"Go on, Moran," I said. "Get the hell out of here and stay out of town until you cool off."

He walked toward the door, glaring at me. "I ain't never gonna cool off, Logan. I needed the sheriff's job. It was the only job I could get that would have given me enough cash money to pay off my debts. If it hadn't been for you, I'd have got it. Nobody else wanted it, but now it goes to a snot-nosed kid who don't have no more idea about how to do his job than a first-grader."

He stood a step from the door, his great shoulders hunched forward. I didn't move. If I let my temper go, I knew what I'd do and there wasn't any sense of adding to my problems at this point.

"Moran," I said, "you'd better get out of here before I lock you up again. You're not doing anything to improve my temper with the kind of talk you're giving me."

"I want my gun," he said.

"You're not getting it," I said. "If I had any notion of giving it to you, I got over it after hearing what you had to say just now."

He started cursing me and I started walking toward him, having had a bellyful of the man. I guess he saw something in my face that convinced him I wasn't just the snot-nosed kid he had called me. He wheeled and strode out into the sunshine, then looked back. He said, his voice quivering, "I ain't done with you, you bastard. You ruined me, and I ain't one to ever forget it."

He swung around again and this time he

strode on around the courthouse toward the street. I stood in the doorway of my office watching him until he disappeared. A nagging thought crossed my mind that I'd made a mistake turning him loose, that I had more reason to worry now with him a free man than when I had him locked up. But I was sure the judge wasn't going to bring charges against him, so I'd have had to turn him loose anyway.

I started toward the hotel, and as I turned the corner of the courthouse, I saw that the judge was coming up the walk. I met him halfway between the street and the front door of the courthouse.

"Good morning, Judge," I said. "You're going to work early."

"Good morning," he said affably. "I don't usually get here this early, but I've got some reading to do this morning. I'm due in Gunnison tomorrow on a case that's got me worried."

"You'll be gone a while?"

He nodded. "I'll have to take the morning stage. The trial starts day after tomorrow. It'll go several days, maybe a week or more."

I felt like saying he couldn't go now, that all hell was going to break loose in a day or two and I would need him. But I didn't. If

I couldn't handle my job without him, I'd better turn in my star this morning.

"I just let Moran loose," I said. "He was breathing fire and brimstone. I'm wondering if I made a mistake."

He shook his head. "No sense in the county giving him free meals. He's more noise than anything else. All smoke, no fire. He'll cool down in a day or two."

He nodded and walked past me and on into the court house. I moved to the street and turned toward the hotel thinking he was dead wrong. Under ordinary circumstances I thought he would have been right about Moran but I had a strong hunch the man was crazy, that it was more than just being sore because he'd lost the sheriff's job.

I didn't know what had turned Moran into a dangerous lunatic, how much he was in debt, or what he meant by my ruining him, but something was clearly wrong and I knew that even the sanest of men can be pushed off the deep end if he's pushed hard enough. It seemed to me that Moran had been pushed that hard.

I intended to get a quick breakfast and saddle up and ride out to Anchor. I wanted to find out for sure if Pappy Jordan really had sold the outfit, but when I stepped into the dining room, I saw the old man having breakfast at a table set against the far wall.

I was astonished because Jordan never, to my knowledge, had breakfast in town. Not that I'd been here for breakfast that often. It was just that I knew it wasn't his style. He seldom, if ever, spent a night away from home. It was mostly, I thought, because he didn't like to leave his wife alone very long, and also because it was cheaper to eat at home. I had often heard it said he was just plain tight, but on the other hand, I knew that in some areas he was a very generous man.

He glanced in my direction, recognized me and motioned for me to join him. He rose when I reached his table, stood up, and extended his hand as he said, "I'm glad you came in. I wanted to see you, partly to congratulate you for being appointed sheriff."

"Thank you, Mr. Jordan." I had never had the temerity to call him Pappy. "Right now I'm not sure I should be congratulated. I guess I stumbled into a hornet's nest I didn't expect."

He motioned to me to sit down and called, "Beulah, bring the sheriff some breakfast."

She came out of the kitchen on the run, her big breasts bouncing. Before she reached our table, she asked, "What'll you have, Ed?"

"Ham and eggs," I said. "Sunny side up. Coffee, too."

"Right away," she said, and, turning, ran back into the kitchen, her rump bouncing as lively as her breasts had.

Jordan leaned forward, his face troubled. "I know, Ed. I didn't know until last night when Caroline Dallas talked to me. She said she'd seen you."

I sat back in my chair and stared at him. I said, "It's true, then, that you did sell Anchor?"

He nodded and started stirring his coffee, his gaze on the black contents of his cup. He said, a little bitterly I thought, "True."

He was a tall man, all long bone and muscle with the fat fried out of him. His lean face was marked deeply by a lifetime spent in the sun and wind. He was a typical cattleman, except that he was one of the old kind who had pioneered the country and had helped tame it: honest, hard-working, his handshake as good as a written contract.

I didn't know his age, but he had settled

in the valley before the first strike was made and was supposed to have built a quick fortune selling beef to the miners. He'd had some hard times since, but he was still a wealthy man.

"How'd the Dallas woman know you were in town?" I asked.

"I spent the night here because Dan Kramer said he'd be in Purgatory today to finish signing the papers and paying the balance of what he owes me for Anchor. I didn't know when he'd be here, and I wanted to get started for Gunnison as soon as I could. I guess she thought I might have come in early and checked the register."

He sipped his coffee, staring at it thoughtfully. "I hadn't told anybody around here that I wanted to sell, but I have been advertising in stockmen's magazines and Dan Kramer saw the ad. I've known him and Caroline's dad for quite a while and always visited with 'em at cattlemen's conventions. I got better acquainted with Dan after the old man got too bunged up to come to the conventions. He never talked much when the old man was around. I always liked both of 'em and it's hard to believe what Caroline says about Dan, but then there ain't no reason for her to lie."

"That's the way I see it," I said. "I guess visiting with a man at a cattleman's convention when he puts his best foot forward is not really knowing the man."

Jordan nodded. "You're right about that."

"You'll be missed in Turner County," I said.

"I expect I will," he said, "and I'll miss everyone here, but I've got to leave. I reckon you knew my wife has been bad with rheumatiz for years. It's got worse lately so she can't hardly get out of bed. She thinks she'll get better in a warm climate. I dunno about that, but we've got to try. She's in Denver now waiting for me. As soon as I get there we'll light out for California."

My breakfast came and Beulah filled Jordan's cup. He had finished eating, but he sat stirring and sipping while I ate. I sensed that he wanted to say more, but I didn't prompt him, figuring he'd get around to saying what he had in mind in his own good time. When I finished and sat back in my chair, he put his cup back into the saucer.

"I made Kramer promise when he was here to keep my crew on," Jordan said, "but now that I've heard what Caroline had to say, I doubt that he'll keep his word."

"He's been here?" I asked, surprised.

"Sure," Jordan nodded. "Looked the whole valley over, which surprised me because Anchor's got all the range it needs. He said he didn't want more range. It was hay land he was after and I didn't have enough. I don't, but hell, I've always bought all I needed from the farmers. It saves me the trouble of fussing with hay and gives them a market. I told him that, but I saw it didn't satisfy him."

He took a long breath, glanced up at me, then turned his gaze back to his coffee cup. "I didn't think too much about it then. I knew your Pa and Gramp Campbell and the rest of 'em wouldn't sell so I figured Kramer would find that out and accept it, but after talking to Caroline, I know he won't. She says he'll kill a couple of 'em and the rest will sell. I suppose they will, but how in hell can he get away with killing a couple of men in cold blood?"

That hit me hard. I put my cup down and rubbed my face. I was into this business over my head. I said, "I dunno, Mr. Jordan, but it sure lays everything right in my lap. I've got to stop him some way. The trouble is he'll be tricky about it, so it'll be hard to prove he's behind the killings."

Jordan nodded. "I'm sure he will. Kramer always seemed such a pleasant man when I'd see him at a convention, but when he was here, and it came right down to bargaining with him, he was a tough bastard. I finally sold for more than he wanted to give and less than I wanted for the outfit, but I didn't have any other offers. With my wife feeling the way she does, I didn't figure I had any choice."

He offered me a cigar and I shook my head. He bit off the end and fired it, then sat back, scowling and puffing. "There's one thing you can do. You know as well as I do that my neighbors have been living on my beef for years. I put up with it, partly because York didn't or couldn't do anything about it, and partly because the loss wasn't enough to really hurt me.

"The truth is I fed 'em because it was easier to do that than to take the law into my own hands. I never was much to do that. If I caught one of 'em red-handed, I don't think I could have strung him up. Dan Kramer can."

He took the pipe out of his mouth and tamped the tobacco down. He went on, "What I want you to do is to talk to every farmer and rancher in the county. Tell them to stop taking Anchor beef. Explain that Anchor has a new owner and rustling his beef will just give him an excuse to rub some of 'em out.

"Kramer asked me if I lost any cattle, if there was any rustling going on. I hemmed and hawed and he saw right through me. He said I was too damned easygoing, but he wasn't. He said he'll hang the first man he catches stealing his beef. From the way he looked when he said it, I figure he will. That's the reason I believe Caroline. I'm sorry I sold to Kramer. It ain't fair to leave the county this way, but I still figure I had no choice, so maybe I'd have done it again if I had it to do over."

"Nobody will blame you," I said. "It's just that we'll miss your influence in county affairs. You're respected as much as Judge Willoughby is."

"I hope so," he said moodily. "One more thing. Kramer had a long talk with Ross the last day he was here. They're two of a kind. As far as their morals go, I mean. Kramer is the kind of man Ross admires, and Ross is the sort of man Kramer can use."

He paused, glancing at me and giving me a ghost of a smile. "I suppose you were surprised when the judge asked you to serve as sheriff. He probably didn't tell you how it happened. When York was killed, the judge came out to see me. We knew Moran wanted the job, but we knew Moran would never stand up to Kramer. We went over every man in the county we could think of and you were the only one we thought could do the job. We informed Ross. We knew the other commissioners would go along with him. He kicked like hell, but he couldn't look us in the face when he said he supported Moran. He finally gave in and said he'd see you got the star."

"I appreciate your support, Mr. Jordan," I said. "I'll do my best."

He rose and held out his hand. "We knew you would. Don't thank me, Ed. Before this is over, you may hate me and the judge. It wasn't just that we wanted to do you a favor. It was self-defense on our part. I couldn't bring myself to leave the county in the hands of Moran."

We shook hands and he left the dining room. Beulah filled my coffee cup, then stood looking down at me. She said, "I was afraid to ask him, but the story's going around that he's sold out and is leaving the county."

I nodded. "It's true."

"Ah me," she sighed. "We'll miss him."

I sat there finishing my coffee, a black mood settling down upon me. I guessed that Caroline Dallas had not told Jordan about Kramer bringing a killer into Turner County or he would have mentioned it. I rose and left the dining room.

As I passed the desk, the clerk called, "Ed, you forgot to pay."

I wheeled on him, suddenly furious. "Beulah told me she'd keep a record and I'd pay at the end of the month."

He stepped back, scared by my outburst. "I'm sorry, Ed. She didn't tell me."

I turned back to the door just as Hubey Zisk, the livery stable boy, ran in from the street. He yelled, "I've been looking for you, Sheriff. Max Moran is roaring drunk and he's looking for you. I thought you ought to know."

"Thanks, Hubey," I said, and moved past him into the street.

Chapter X

I heard Moran yelling before I was through the doorway. His voice was high-pitched and strident, crazy-sounding, as if he was out of his head which he probably was. I didn't see how he could possibly have gotten this drunk in the short time since I had released him from jail.

"Where's that son of a bitch of a kid sheriff?" he screamed. "I'm gonna kill the bastard."

He held a gun over his head and fired at the sky. People had appeared from the stores and places of business to see what was going on. I paused on the boardwalk a moment, wondering if I ought to go back into the hotel and wait until he ran down. Then I knew I couldn't do that. He wasn't hurting anyone now, but he might if I let him go on shooting and cursing the way he was doing. He was completely irresponsible, and if I didn't show up, he might turn his gun on someone else. I couldn't risk that, so I moved into the street.

"Drop your gun, Moran," I shouted.

"You're under arrest for disturbing the peace."

"So you finally crawled out from under a rock, did you, Logan?" Moran stood in the front of the livery stable. Now he started toward me, brandishing a .45. "Oh, I'll drop my gun, all right, just as soon as I put a couple of windows in your skull."

I stood motionless in the middle of the street, my gun in my hand. He shot at me, the bullet going ten feet over my head. "I don't want to kill you, Max," I yelled. "Don't make me do it. Now drop your gun."

He fired again, the bullet kicking up dust in front of me. I knew I wasn't going to be able to stand any more of this, that he wasn't hearing anything I said. Maybe he couldn't. Maybe he was that crazy, but crazy or not, he was like a mad dog and I knew he would kill me if I let him.

I heard men shouting at me, first Mark Vance's voice, "Shoot him, Ed," and Caleb Watts's, "Don't stand there and let him kill you." His third shot hit me then, opening a gash along my left side under my arm. It felt as if someone had pulled a hot branding iron along my ribs.

Moran started to run, closing the gap between us. Bud Campbell and I had practiced with our six-guns as often as we could afford to buy shells, so I was reasonably accurate, accurate enough to make me think I could wing him and make him drop his gun. I aimed to hit his right arm, but the slug didn't go where I aimed. Judging from the way he went down, I had killed him.

I stood motionless, shocked into a sort of paralysis by what I had been forced to do. I knew that no one would ever believe I had not intended to kill Moran. He lay motionless, his hat in the dust beside his head, his gun a few inches from the end of his outstretched fingers.

The sound of gunfire had been like thunder rolling across the valley, echoing and reechoing off the false fronts of Main Street. Then there was a short period of shocked silence, and a few seconds later Doc Wardell pushed through the crowd and ran to where Moran lay.

I paced forward slowly, not even then fully grasping what had happened in these last few seconds. When I reached Moran, Wardell had rolled him over onto his back. He felt of Moran's pulse and shook his head. When he stood up, a crowd had gathered around us.

"Dead, ain't he?" Vance asked.

Wardell nodded. "Dead as he'll ever be. Ed's slug must have blown his heart apart."

Simon Ross had rammed his way through the crowd. He grabbed me by an arm and shook me. "You've gone too far, Logan. Turn in your star, you murdering son of a bitch. I knew you weren't man enough to handle the job."

Caleb Watts yanked him away from me. "Looks to me like he was plenty of man. What did you expect him to do, Simon? Stand there and let Moran smoke him down?"

Vance took Ross by an arm and started dragging him away. "Come on, Simon. You belong in your bank, not out here."

Wardell motioned to the bartender from the hotel. "Fetch that door you keep in the back room, Luke. Get some men to help you tote him over to my office."

I stood away from the others, trembling and sweating, a strange feeling of being apart from all of this taking hold of me. I had killed a man, and yet somehow it seemed as if it hadn't been me at all, but someone else in my body, and I was floating above this scene with the lingering smell of gunsmoke and horse manure and dust and the small puddle of mud that the blood flowing from Moran's chest made in the street dirt.

I guess Caleb just then noticed the dark spot that had stained my shirt. He yelled. "Hey, Doc, Ed's been hit."

Wardell looked at me in surprise. "By God, so he has. Why didn't you say so? Come on into my office and we'll take a look at it."

He jerked his head toward his office, a small, frame building on the bank side of the street. I followed, Caleb walking beside me. The crowd was scattering. Nobody said anything to me until I reached the walk in front of Wardell's office. Charlie Lambert stood there looking at me as if he couldn't believe what he had seen.

When I reached Lambert, he said, "You handled your iron real well, Logan. Real well."

I hadn't realized until then that I was still holding my gun at my side. I holstered it, and followed Wardell into his office, Caleb a step behind me. Wardell motioned toward a long, narrow table as he said, "Pull your shirt off, Ed, and I'll see what kind of a hole you've got."

Not until that moment did I realize that the wound was burning like hell. I was back on earth again, conscious of my body which was hurting. So was my soul, or conscience, or whatever it is that hammers the truth at a man that he has done a terrible thing.

I guess Caleb sensed that. He put a hand on my shoulder as he said, "You had to do what you did, Ed. He'd have killed you if you hadn't."

"He sure as hell would," Wardell said. "I thought for what seemed an eternity that you were going to stand there and let him do it."

I had my shirt off by that time and sat on the side of the table. Wardell studied the wound and grinned. "Well, son, you ain't hurt bad at all. It's shallow, which surprises me a little the way it's bleeding. We'll fix it so you won't keep bleeding on your clothes, but I can't keep it from hurting for a day or two. You're lucky. An inch or two farther in and you'd have some sore ribs and maybe some busted ones."

He splashed something on the wound that stung enough to make me grunt, then he bandaged it. He turned to his cupboard, took down a bottle and poured a stiff drink into a glass.

"Get this down," he said. "You look like you're going to topple over when you stand up."

I took the glass and drank the stuff he'd poured into it. I don't know what it was, but it had a hell of a wallop. I felt better. I rose from the table and staggered across the office and sat down in a chair. I'd quit trembling. I took my bandanna out of my pocket and wiped my face. I discovered I wasn't sweating.

"I don't know what got into Moran," I said. "I let him out of jail this morning. I'd locked him up last night because he threatened the judge, but I figured the judge wasn't going to press charges, so I turned him loose. He couldn't have got that drunk in an hour or two."

"I don't think he did," Caleb said. "It's my guess he was already crazy, and a drink or two just set him off."

"I should have known he'd gone loco," I said. "He acted crazy yesterday when he tried to kill the judge, then today when I let him out of jail, he didn't act right. I kept thinking he'd cool off if he got out of town."

"He never left town," Caleb said. "He went into some saloon — I don't know which one — and the meanness in him just built up to the exploding point."

"Nobody's gonna miss him except Simon Ross," the doctor said. "Did you see the way Mark Vance hauled Simon back into the bank?" He chuckled. "It did me good to see Mark get some backbone into him. He's had Simon telling him how to run his store ever since his daddy died."

"I wish I knew who the bartender was that gave Moran the whisky," I said. "I'd run him out of town."

"It's not likely you'll find out," Caleb said, "but if you do, you won't run him out of town. You can't really blame him, whoever he was. He didn't know what Moran would do. Liquor does different things with different people."

"I know you're right," I said, "but it still makes me mad. I can't see what made Moran blow up. I never thought much of him, and neither did Pa, but we always figured he was more or less harmless."

"I think I know what happened," Caleb said. "He told me this in confidence, but now that he's dead, I think it will be all right if I tell you. He never came to church much, though he belonged. I knew who he was and that's about all.

"A few days ago he stopped by the parsonage and wanted to talk to me. I was flabbergasted. He'd never done anything like that before. When he did come to church, he sat in the back pew and was the first one out of the building. I took him back to my study and the first thing he said was to ask me what happened to people who killed themselves.

"He said there wasn't any use for him to go on living, that nobody cared. He couldn't do business around here any more. No one would dicker with him and he couldn't sell his horses and he was in debt —"

"Oh hell," Wardell interrupted. "He had no one to blame but himself. He's cheated every man in the county. What did he expect?"

"I know," Caleb said. "He swindled me once on a horse trade, but he didn't mention that and I didn't remind him. Anyhow, he said he'd been gambling in Gunnison and owed a lot of money to one of the cardsharps. He didn't have any way to pay his debts and he was getting pressured. I have never seen a man as depressed as he was. He acted like he had no place to turn, so it strikes me he simply didn't have any choice but to provoke you into killing him."

"What did you tell him about what happens to people who commit suicide?" Wardell asked.

"Oh, the Bible makes that plain

enough," Caleb said. "A man goes to hell. It's a mortal sin to take your own life."

"I thought you'd say that," Wardell said testily. "I don't agree. I've seen cases where taking his life saved a man a lot of suffering. I don't agree that it's a —" He stopped and shrugged his shoulders. "Oh hell, I learned a long time ago that there's no use arguing with a preacher."

I was only half listening. I remembered what he had said about me taking the sheriff's job, that he would have had it if I hadn't got it. It made some sense to me, but I still had no inkling about why Ross had supported him for the office. It seemed to me that a banker more than anyone else would want a competent sheriff. Of course he had no way of knowing whether I'd be competent, but at least it seemed that I'd be a better bet than Moran, but I didn't raise the point with Wardell and Caleb.

"I guess there isn't," Caleb laughed. "Not that we know it all, but I guess we preachers sometimes act that way, particularly if it comes to a point of what the Bible teaches."

Wardell was willing to drop the argument. He turned to me. "Ed, I guess you know that some folks were thinking you wouldn't work out as sheriff because you're young and inexperienced, but it's my guess that they know now you've got the guts to do the job."

"That's right," Caleb said. "I think you'll get plenty of support if you need it."

"I think I will," I said.

I stood up and remained motionless for a moment, feeling dizzy. I wasn't sure whether it was due to my wound, the drink Doc had given me, or the aftermath of having killed a man. In a few seconds the dizziness left me, but the bullet wound stung like hell.

Wardell must have known that because he said, "That scratch ain't going to bother you long. It'll start to heal in a day or two."

"I hope so," I said. "Thanks, Doc."

Several men were carrying Moran's body into Wardell's office as I left. I don't know what they'd been doing all this time, but I guessed that the bartender couldn't find the door they used to carry bodies off the street. It hadn't been used for months, maybe years, but from what I'd heard, a killing in the street had been a common occurrence in the mining days.

I was surprised to see Hubey Zisk waiting outside Wardell's office. He fell into step beside me, asking, "You all right, Sheriff?"

I nodded. "I'm fine."

Hubey had been a little kid when I'd been a senior in school. He had hung around the baseball diamond when we were practicing and chased flies for us. He had been a sort of pest, wanting to be with Bud Campbell or me or any of the other big boys, and sometimes we'd chased him off when we got tired of having him around. I hadn't seen much of him after I graduated, but I knew he'd been a poor student and had dropped out of school to go to work in the livery stable.

We started walking toward the livery stable. Hubey kept looking at me, then looking away. I sensed that nothing had changed since high school. I guess it had been a sort of hero worship with him when I'd been the catcher on the baseball team, and it was the same with him now.

"Sheriff," he burst out when we were almost across the street. "I hope to hell you ain't hurt bad. I was scared when Moran kept shooting and you stood there making a damn big target. I don't want to see you killed. A lot of other folks don't, either. You're what this county needs."

I stopped in front of the livery stable and

stood looking down at the boy's eager face. Hero worship or not, there was nothing in the world I needed to hear right then more than the words he'd just said.

"Thanks, Hubey," I said. "Saddle Alexander up for me. I've got to do some riding."

"You bet, Sheriff," Hubey said and, wheeling, ran into the stable.

I went on to my house, put on a clean shirt, rolled up my bloodied ones and left the house. I'd take my clothes to Ma, who knew how to clean up the blood spots. A minute or so later I was in the saddle and headed out of town, one thought pounding through my head. I would never tell anyone that it had been by sheer accident that I had killed Moran through the heart. Let people think I was a regular Deadeye Dick. A reputation like that might save me a hell of a lot of trouble later on.

Chapter XI

The full impact of what I had done didn't hit me until I was out of town and alone. I suppose my mind had nudged the fact that I had killed a man into a back corner of my consciousness. When I was alone with no one to talk to and nothing to divert my thoughts it hit me like a hard blow in the belly.

The mental picture of Max Moran lying in the dust, the morning sun on his motionless body, his hat beside him in the dirt, blood flowing out of the bullet hole I had given him: All made a morbid picture that would not go away.

I was going to be sick. I could feel it starting in the very bottom of my belly and moving up. I reined off the road and angled across a pasture to the river. When I reached the fringe of willows that bordered the stream, I dismounted and staggered toward the bank. I threw up before I reached the water, then, gasping for breath, I lay down on a sand bar at the edge of a riffle.

I don't know how long I lay there. The sun had lifted into the sky and the day grew warm. I wasn't unconscious, but I wasn't doing any thinking, either. Then, as if by magic, the tragic events of the morning were driven out of my mind by a new thought: My father might be dead by this time tomorrow. I had been lying on my back, an arm thrown over my eyes. Now I sat upright, knowing I had to tell Pa what was happening. He was too stubborn to pay any attention to my warning. I didn't have the slightest idea how I could make him go into hiding or take any steps to prevent his murder.

I rose, slapped the sand off my shirt and pants the best I could, and jammed my way through the willow jungle to the pasture where I had left Alexander. I stopped, seeing to my surprise that I was directly opposite the Campbell buildings.

For a crazy moment I seemed to have a glimpse of the future, of Gramp Campbell lying in front of his house dead, with Bud and his grandmother bending over him. If I had the right hunch about Buck Sharkey, he would hide in the willows until he had a clear view of Gramp Campbell, then he'd shoot him, get back on his horse, and ride off, holding close to the willows until he was far enough away so he wouldn't be recognized.

I stepped into the saddle and rode straight for the Campbell house. Bud and his grandfather had butchered a steer. The carcass was hanging from a big limb of a cottonwood that grew back of the house. Bud saw me first and let out a whoop.

"Get down and rest your saddle, you old horse thief," Bud yelled. "Ain't seen you for a coon's age. What have you been up to?" Then he noticed I was carrying my gun. He raised his gaze to my chest and saw the star, then shook his head in amazement. "What are you doing, playing Cowboys and Indians?"

"Not hardly," I said. "I'm the new sheriff of Turner County. Sheriff York is dead."

They had been skinning the beef. The old man had kept right on working, not even nodding a greeting at me, but now he stopped and turned to stare at me. They looked a lot alike, or would have if Bud had been fifty years older. They were big men, red-haired, with blue eyes and jutting chins, but the older Campbell's shoulders were bent, his beard and mustache more white than red, the skin of his face wrinkled and discolored by brown splotches.

Bud was within a week of my age. His face held more freckles per square inch than anyone else I had ever seen. When we'd been kids, Bud had been an active boy who could think up more deviltry in a minute than I could in a couple of days. I'd got into trouble more than once by going along with some of his antics.

We hadn't seen much of each other lately, mostly, I think because I had grown up and Bud hadn't. He was still the crazy, rambunctious kid he had been when we were in school, and I'd decided that it wasn't any fun figuring out some practical joke and laughing my head off when our victim could have been hurt. In fact, I'd reached the point where I was ashamed of many of the things we had done that we'd thought were funny.

They stood motionless and speechless for a good thirty seconds, then Bud said, "Aw hell, Ed, what do you take us for? That's the biggest pile of bull you ever shoveled. They wouldn't give the star to a fellow your age."

"Well, they did," I said, my impatience growing. "I've got bad news. Pappy Jordan has sold out to a man name Dan Kramer. Pappy's leaving the valley today."

It was plain from the expression on the old man's face that he thought I was lying. He said sourly, "I don't know what kind of a trick you're trying to play on us, Ed. I thought you'd outgrowed that stuff. I knowed Bud was still about fifteen years old, but I didn't think you were."

The remark irritated Bud. He said, "Damn it, Gramp, I'm getting sick of you —"

"That's not the bad news," I interrupted. "I hope you'll start believing me, Mr. Campbell, because your life's on the line. We've never had a man like Kramer in the county before. Not in my memory anyway. He's hired a killer. He wants the whole valley, your place and ours and all the rest. He'll buy them, I understand, but if you won't sell, he'll see that you're a dead man. He figures that one or two killings will convince the rest that he means business and they'll sell."

The old man turned his back to me and started skinning again. Bud didn't move. He kept staring at me, not sure whether I was lying or not, but he knew me better than the old man did, and I thought he was believing me. I jerked my head at him and rode toward the front of the house. He followed me, reluctantly, it seemed, scowling as if he couldn't make up his mind about me.

When I reined up, he said, "Ed, if you're bulling me, I'm gonna —"

"I'm not," I said. "I fell into a damned hornet's nest and I don't know how I'll stop Buck Sharkey."

"Sharkey?" He practically yelled the word at me. "I suppose you're seeing all kinds of ghosts and goblins and ogres. You used to like reading about them."

"I still do," I said. "Now shut up and listen. This man Kramer is coming to town today. I don't know if Sharkey is here yet or not. I'll jail both of 'em if I can find anything to charge them with, but right now I don't have anything. I had breakfast with Pappy Jordan this morning in the hotel, and he admitted as much about this business as he knew. I don't know if you can convince your grandpa that I'm telling the truth, but keep him under cover as much as you can. It's my guess Sharkey will try to dry gulch him from the willows. It's close enough for a man who's a good shot to drill him from there without giving any warning."

Bud shook his head. "By God, Ed, you don't look drunk, but you sure as hell must be."

He turned on his heel and stalked back to where his grandpa was working with his skinning knife. I sat in my saddle for a few seconds, a feeling of absolute failure working through me. I had intended to ask Bud to serve as deputy if I needed him, but I decided it would only be a waste of time, so I touched Alexander up and rode down the lane to the county road.

I guess I had known all the time that no one would believe me, but I didn't think I would be given the curt dismissal I had just received, one of sheer contempt. Pa would be the same, I thought glumly. That's the way it would be with everyone on the North Fork. It would take some killings to convince them that Kramer meant what he was saying, or would be saying as soon as he got here, and that wasn't going to help the first ones Kramer used as object lessons.

When I rode into our yard a few minutes later, I looked at the house that needed painting, the weather-beaten barn and sheds and corrals, at our old milk cow Susie grazing in the pasture beyond the corrals, and I had the weird feeling that I had been gone for months instead of only a few hours.

I stripped gear from Alexander, watered him at the trough beside the barn and turned him into one of the corrals. It was nearly noon and I knew I could scrounge dinner off Ma. Carrying the bundle of blood-stained clothes, I walked toward the house, aiming to go through the back door, but, before I stepped up on the porch, I saw that Pa was moving the wood we had sawed up the day before yesterday to the woodshed.

I dropped my clothes on the porch and walked on past the woodshed to where Pa was loading the wheelbarrow. He looked up just as he placed a block of wood on the wheelbarrow, paused a second, and said, "Looks like you came home for a good meal."

"Something like that," I said. "Actually I came to give you some bad news."

He started to push the wheelbarrow toward the wood shed, saying "Like what?"

"I shot and killed Max Moran this morning," I said.

He stopped, stared at me, then lowered the wheelbarrow to the ground. He walked back to the woodpile, set a chunk on end and sat down. He got his pipe and can of Prince Albert out of his pocket and dribbled tobacco into the bowl. The irrelevant thought struck me that I had never before in my life seen Pa quit in the middle of a job. He always managed to talk and work at the same time.

"How did it happen?" he asked.

After I told him, he said, "Well, but it wasn't none of your fault. I'd say you couldn't have done anything else."

"He'd have killed me if I hadn't killed him," I said, "but that doesn't make me feel any better."

"No, I reckon it wouldn't," he said, puffing on his pipe. "I never killed a man, though I've come close a time or two. I guess that if I had, I'd feel the same way you do."

"There's something else that makes me feel worse," I said.

I told him the whole story about Pappy Jordan selling out and Dan Kramer buying Anchor and what he intended to do. I thought he would take it the way Gramp Campbell had but I was wrong. He didn't say a word for at least a minute. He just sat motionless puffing on his pipe and staring at the willow jungle along the North Fork, then he took the pipe out of his mouth and tamped the tobacco down.

"That sure is a hell of a situation," he said. "I wouldn't have been surprised if this had happened in the boom days, but now?" He shook his head. "It puts you between the rock and a hard place, don't it?"

I'd lived with Pa for twenty-one years; I'd known him as a hard worker, a man who was often intolerant of failure in others, a practical man who had always demanded the best from me and had been rarely satisfied. Now for the first time in my life he was understanding. Suddenly it occurred to me that I was accepted as an adult simply because I had taken a demanding job and had left home.

"It does for a fact," I said, "but what concerns me is how to protect you and others. If I catch up with Sharkey, I'll handle him some way, but I can't spend the next several weeks patrolling the river. He'd know it if I did and he'd try killing you from somewhere else." I nodded toward the west. "He could get close enough up there on the ridge among those rocks to shoot you and you'd never know he was there. And he has a special reason to get you with me being sheriff."

He pulled on his pipe, found that it had gone cold and knocked it out against his boot heel. "I was never one to worry about what might happen, but I'll keep my eyes open. I can't let the work pile up and go hide. You know that, and you know I won't sell out because a bastard like this Kramer fellow threatens me."

"I was sure you wouldn't," I said, "but I had to warn you and hope you'd stay under cover as much as you can."

"I will." He rose and put a hand on my shoulder, the first time I ever remembered him doing anything that resembled a show of affection. "Thanks for coming out. Now let's go see what Ma's fixed to eat."

We went into the house through the back door, my bundle of bloodied clothes in my hand. Ma cried out in delight when she saw me, and said she'd put on another plate and throw a third slice of ham into the frying pan. Then she asked what the clothes were and I had to tell her what had happened. She didn't cry, but I thought she was going to.

"I'll do the best I can with them," she said, then she stood looking at me as she brushed back a stray strand of gray hair. "I don't like it, Ed. I don't like it one bit."

The atmosphere was strained as we ate dinner. I didn't tell Ma about Kramer and Sharkey. It would only give her something else to worry about. Pa could tell her if he wanted to, but I didn't think he would. I knew very well that there was nothing Ma could do to make Pa stay inside the house.

As soon as we finished eating, I said I had to get back to town. I went into my room and made up a bundle of clean clothes. When I left, Ma kissed me and said to be as careful as I could. I promised that I would. Pa walked with me to the corral and watched while I saddled Alexander.

He didn't give me any advice, but after I'd climbed aboard, he said, "If you need any help getting up a posse or something like that, just give a holler." He hesitated, then he asked, "Think there's any connection between the way Moran performed and this Kramer business?"

"I don't see how there could be," I said, "but it's damned peculiar."

"That's what I was thinking," he said.

I lifted a hand in farewell, then rode away, glad he had at least been warned and wondering if I would ever see him again. I had a hunch the same thought was in his mind.

Chapter XII

The instant I rode through the archway of the livery stable, Hubey Zisk saw me and dropped what he was doing. He ran down the runway toward me, his eyes bright with excitement. "There's a new man in town, Sheriff," Hubey said. "Rode in about an hour ago." He nodded at a big roan in one of the stalls. "That's his horse. Looked like he'd been ridden purty hard. He told me to water him and rub him down, then give him a double bait of oats. He gave me a dollar tip and said he'd pay his bill when he left which wouldn't be for a couple of days."

I looked at the roan, then at Hubey, and asked, "What's so important about this fellow riding into town?"

"He's different, Sheriff," Hubey said. "He's tall and bow-legged, and he's wearing fancy cowboy duds like a damn greenhorn. He sure ain't no ordinary cowpoke. He's a gunslick. I never seen a man like him. My daddy was one of the first to settle in the valley and I've heard him tell about men like this one, but we sure don't see 'em these days." He took a long breath, then said anxiously, "Think you can take him, Sheriff?"

I had never seen Hubey worked up as much as he was right then, not even when we beat the Gunnison town team two to one on my home run in the last of the ninth. "I don't aim to find out," I said. "I've had enough gunfighting for today. What makes you so sure he's a gunslick?"

"He's packing two guns," Hubey said. "He's carrying 'em tied down butts forward. I never seen anything like it."

I had never seen a two-gun man; and I never had seen a gun carried butt forward, either. The man could be Buck Sharkey, I thought dismally, and I had to find out if I could take him whether I had my fill of gunfighting or not. I said, "Thanks, Hubey." I started toward the street, but paused when Hubey hollered, "Hey, I almost forgot. Mark Vance wants to see you. He came in about an hour ago and said he'd been looking all over for you. He told me to tell you to come to the store as soon as you got back."

"He'll have to wait," I said, and went on through the archway to the street.

I was curious about why Vance wanted to see me as much as Hubey said he did, but there was nothing that the storekeeper knew and wanted to tell me that matched Buck Sharkey's appearance in town, if the stranger was Sharkey as I was convinced he was. It was simply too much of a coincidence for a gunman to show up in town at this particular time.

I started looking for him, first in the hotel dining room, then in the bar, but he wasn't in either. I asked Beulah if she'd seen a man who answered the description Hubey had given me, and she said he'd had his dinner and had just left.

I figured he'd be in one of the saloons, so I headed for Clancy's bar. All the time I was hunting for him, I was also doing some fast thinking. I wasn't sure of my legal grounds, and Judge Willoughby wasn't here to give me any answers, but I knew damned well I couldn't beat a man like Sharkey to the draw if it came to that, so I'd keep it from going that far. One thing was sure. I was going to get him out of town, if I had to make up something to charge him with.

He wasn't in Clancy's place, but he was in the Cattlemen's Rest across the street. I spotted him before I pushed through the bat-wings. He was standing with his back to the door, one hand on the bar. He was talking to a man named Sid Wallop, a small rancher who lived about five miles downstream from us. He wore two guns, all right, butts forward, his battered black Stetson thumbed to the back of his head.

I hadn't made up my mind how I was going to take him, but when I saw him with his back to me, intent on his conversation with Wallop, I made up my mind in a hurry. I drew my gun, pulled the hammer back, and eased through the bat-wings softly and slowly so I wouldn't make a sound. He was talking up a storm, waving his right hand around to emphasize what he was saying. I cat-footed straight to the man and had my gun muzzle in the small of his back before he knew I was in the room.

"Don't move," I said. "I'm the sheriff. My gun goes off mighty easy."

He stopped in the middle of a sentence and stood motionless. Wallop stared at me as if I had gone out of my mind. He bellowed, "What the hell's wrong with you, Logan? I heard you was appointed sheriff. It's gone to your head, looks like. This man was just talking to —"

"Shut up, Wallop," I said. "Mister, don't try any fast moves. I want you to draw your left hand gun easy like and lay it on the bar. Then put the other gun beside it."

He didn't move for several seconds. The back of his suntanned neck turned as red as it could. I jabbed him with my gun. "Move, damn it, before you get your backbone sliced in two."

"Sheriff," he said, "I don't know who you think I am, but I'm not wanted by the law. I just rode into town —"

"And now you're riding out," I said. "I'm not famous for my patience. Do what I tell you."

He still hesitated, so I jabbed him again, harder this time. The bartender had been watching, a disapproving scowl on his face. Now he moved forward so that he stood directly across the bar from us. He said, "Ed, you're —"

"I don't want either advice or interference, Rusty," I said, "so stay out of it."

Slowly the man drew one gun and laid it on the bar, then the other. He muttered, "Now what?"

"Rusty, take care of his guns for the time being," I said. "I'll pick them up later. Now mister, what's your name?"

"Buck," he answered sullenly. "Buck Smith."

"All right, Mister Smith," I said. "Head for the door. We're taking a walk."

"If you're taking me in," he said as he turned to face me, "I've got a right to know what the charge is."

Now that I had a chance to see his face, I was shocked. He was the meanest-looking man I had ever seen in my life. He had an eagle beak of a nose, eyes so colorless I could hardly make out their pale blue, and a hideous scar down his right cheek that curved toward his mouth so he seemed to have a perpetual half-smile. The left side of his face had a large red splotch — a birth mark, I judged — that added to his repulsive appearance.

I knew I had to find some kind of charge, legal or not, but I hadn't thought of one. Now, off the top of my head, I said, I'm arresting you for carrying two guns. We haven't had any trouble in Purgatory for a long time. I'm the only man who is allowed to go armed."

Rusty started to sputter something about there wasn't any such law. I was getting damned sore, first about Wallop, then the bartender, both questioning what I was doing. I didn't have time to explain anything to them. I figured that if I could get the man out of town, I was doing all I could.

I knew I didn't have anything to jail him

for, but maybe I could make him decide to leave the county. It was a forlorn hope, but it was all I had. Too, I was giving myself some time to figure out what to do.

"Rusty," I said, "if you don't shut your God-damned mouth, I'll throw you into the jug for interfering with me in my performance of duty."

I made that up, too, but he subsided after muttering something about me being mighty high-handed. My prisoner decided he wasn't to get any help, so he started toward the door. I followed about two paces behind. We marched down the street that way. The people on the boardwalks stopped to stare at us, but no one interfered.

When we were opposite the livery stable, I said, "Turn in here, Smith."

Hubey Zisk was standing in the archway watching us, his mouth hanging open in astonishment. I called, "Hubey, saddle the man's horse, then saddle Alexander."

"You bet, Sheriff," Hubey said, and wheeled and ran into the stable and on back to the stall that held the roan.

He waited in the runway until Hubey saddled the roan and led him to Smith who took the reins. When Hubey brought Alexander, I mounted and ordered Smith to do the same, then I said, "Ride north. Now get moving."

A moment later we were out of town, my gun still in my hand. The people on the street stopped to watch this scene, too. I thought that the excitement hadn't even started, but already more had happened today in Purgatory than had happened in the past ten years.

When we were well out of town, I asked, "What are you doing here, Smith?"

"I'm looking for work," he answered sullenly.

"What kind?"

"A riding job."

"I never saw a working cowboy carry two guns," I said. "Usually they don't even carry one."

"I always carry two," he said sullenly. "I've got some enemies."

We didn't say anything more until we reached the lower end of the valley. I reined up just below where the road started its looping climb over the mountain that closed off this end of the valley. The river turned northwest and cut through the mountain, making what we called the Narrows, a gorge with walls so steep that there was no room for a road along the water.

"Keep going, Smith," I said. "Keep

going right on over the ridge all the way to Gunnison. Don't show your face in Purgatory again."

He reined up and hipped around in the saddle to glare at me, his face uglier than ever. "You make the laws back there in that stinking little burg?"

"I make the ones for men who come to town carrying two guns," I said.

He said in an ominous tone, "I'll be back. You can count on it. I'll get my hands on a gun and that tin star you're packing won't do you one damn bit of good."

He rode on. I watched him until he disappeared around a bend in the road. I figured he would be back, all right. I had a nagging feeling I should have jailed him, but I didn't have any legal excuse, so if I had, Judge Willoughby would have skinned me for making my own laws.

I reined around and rode back to town, uneasy but convinced I had done all I could. I had a little time. Smith probably wouldn't be back for another day or two. I'd probably see Dan Kramer today and I'd at least have a chance to tell him I was onto his game and I'd hold him responsible for any killings we had in the valley. Maybe he'd pull in his horns. Not likely, but maybe, and right then I realized I was reaching for a lot of maybes.

I stopped at the Cattlemen's Rest and picked up Smith's guns. Rusty gave me a sour look as he handed the Colts to me. "You're young, Logan, and the star's gone to your head. You keep acting high and mighty as you done with that Smith hombre, and you're gonna lose your job."

"Don't tell Simon Ross," I said. "He wants my star already."

I rode to the jail and locked the guns in the gun cabinet, then rode back to the livery stable. Hubey was on hand to greet me again. He asked, "You kill him, Sheriff?"

"You're a bloodthirsty fellow," I said. "Why would I kill him?"

"I figured he was the kind who'd resist arrest," Hubey said. "Besides, I'd feel safer with him dead. He's a scary one."

"Well, all I did was to see he got out of town and I told him to stay out," I said.

I handed the reins to Hubey and started to walk out when Hubey said, "Oh, I almost forgot. Mark Vance was back again and kicked my ass all over the stable for not sending you over to the store. He's sure wanting to see you, Sheriff. You'd better tend to it or he won't believe I told you."

"Oh hell," I said. "I'd forgotten all about

him. All right, Hubey, I'll go see him."

As I crossed the street to the Mercantile, I thought sourly that I had enough worries without Vance adding to them. I didn't figure he had anything good to tell me or he wouldn't have been so insistent on seeing me. Maybe he was going to tell me what a great man Simon Ross was. That wouldn't be anything I wanted to hear, either.

Chapter XIII

Vance was arranging cans of fruit on a shelf in the back of the store when I went in. The minute the door closed behind me he turned from the shelf and strode toward me, shouting, "Where the hell have you been?"

I stopped, glared at him, then turned and started to walk out. "Hold on," he said, his voice still loud but not intimidating as it had been. "I've got something to tell you and I've been to the livery stable twice to tell Hubey to send you over here."

"He told me twice," I said, stopping with my hand on the door knob. "I couldn't come the first time. I had some urgent business to attend to and I just got back in town. Now I'm here. What's on your mind?"

He knew I was sore. I figured he was still thinking of me as a kid who wasn't responsible enough to have a star on my shirt. I was getting damned tired of that attitude. He stopped about ten feet from the door and chewed on his lower lip for a few seconds. I thought he was going to ask me what my urgent business was and I wasn't going to tell him. I didn't want everyone in town knowing what was brewing, and I was convinced that no one would believe it until something happened like having Pa or one of his neighbors shot.

Right now I had to play it that way until I saw exactly what the game was. I believed what Caroline Dallas and Pappy Jordan had said, and this fellow Buck Smith or whatever his name was showing up today didn't strike me as being coincidence, but still no actual crime had been committed, so I wasn't sure. I guess that running Smith out of town was about the most illegal act that had been committed.

He stared at me for a few seconds as if he couldn't make up his mind about me, then he shrugged his shoulders and jerked his head at me. "Come on back and sit down. I can work and talk at the same time."

I followed him along the aisle to the cracker-barrel in the back. I sat down on an upended nail keg and helped myself to a handful of crackers. He opened a bottle of soda pop and handed it to me. Then he asked abruptly, "What do you know about the woman who came in on the stage yesterday?"

"Caroline Dallas?" I asked, surprised.

I wondered what he was getting at. He knew she had asked me to come to her room, and I felt another wave of anger wash through me as the notion struck me that maybe he thought she was a whore and had invited me to her room to offer me some free service so she could start up a business.

I had never been very far away from Purgatory, so didn't know how it was in the rest of the world, but here people always figured something was going on if a man visited a woman in her hotel room, even when it was an official, like me.

Vance kept stacking cans on the shelf as he said, "I don't know what her name is. I knew you'd seen her after she got in yesterday and I'd like to know what she's doing here."

"She didn't take me into her confidence," I said.

He turned to face me. "I don't like the smell of some things that have been happening, mostly because I don't know what they mean. That woman came in this morning and bought a double-barreled, twelve-gauge shotgun and a box of shells. Now I want you to tell me why a young woman who hasn't been in town twenty-four hours needs a shotgun and a box of shells."

"I don't have the slightest idea," I said. "She didn't tell me she was buying a shotgun. Maybe she's going hunting."

"For what?" he snorted in disgust. "I wondered why she bought a twelve gauge. It'll knock her on her ass the first time she fires it."

"I'm guessing she knows guns," I said, deciding it was safe to tell him that much. "She grew up on a ranch near Trinidad."

"The hell." He drew a cigar out of his pocket and bit off the end, then fired it. "She don't look like a ranch girl."

"She's been a teacher in Denver for some time," I said, "so she probably lost her ranch look, if there is such a thing. Maybe she wants to buy an outfit around here. Her father died recently. He had a big spread judging from what she said."

He puffed thoughtfully on his cigar, then he said, "Buying a shotgun is a funny way to start looking for a ranch. Something else happened that may or may not be connected with her. It ain't as peculiar as her buying the shotgun. The fellow that rode in on the stage with her came in early this morning and bought a .30-.30 and a box of shells. Later I saw him ride out of town on a livery stablehorse."

He started pacing back and forth along the aisle, puffing hard on his cigar. I said, "I think I can explain that. His name's Charlie Lambert. He said he was going into the mountains and asked me about wild animals and outlaws. He told me he was going to buy a rifle."

Vance wheeled around and faced me, his legs spread. He said, "Ed, it just don't add up right to me. You know how it's been here. For weeks we don't have nobody ride into town or come in on the stage. I mean, no strangers except drummers and these people sure as hell ain't drummers. Now we have two of 'em on the same stage and they both buy guns the same day. It just figures there's something that ain't right. There's got to be a connection. I don't like it worth a damn."

I wondered what he'd say if I told him about Buck Smith riding into town, making a total of three strangers who apparently had no connection with each other. The chances were he hadn't seen the man and he certainly didn't know I'd moved the fellow out of town.

"I don't like it, either," I said, "but I've already found out that as sheriff I can't do a thing until a crime has been committed.

Even if this pair is up to something, what can we do?"

"I dunno Ed," he said gloomily, "I wish I did."

"Thanks for telling me about them," I said. "I think I'll go talk to the Dallas woman. Meanwhile, keep your eyes open."

I walked out, a little surprised that Mark Vance was this concerned about the community's welfare. I had more or less put him in Simon Ross's class, but I realized I had a lot to learn about the people I was sworn to protect. I had just learned something about the storekeeper.

When I angled across the street, I noticed that among the various rigs tied in front of the hotel and store and the saloons was a buckboard and a team of horses I had never seen before. I glanced back at the buckboard just before I entered the lobby and noticed that half a dozen valises and one trunk were piled behind the seat. As I stepped up on the boardwalk, the thought struck me that we must have at least one more stranger in town. I wondered what Vance would make of that.

I was inside the lobby and halfway across it when I was aware of a strange woman sitting in a chair with her back to the window. I came close to stopping and staring at her when I realized she was abnormally fat, and I remembered Caroline saying that her sister had been too fat to have any beaus when she was a girl.

I don't think I broke stride as I crossed the lobby. I didn't want to embarrass the woman by staring at her, but the thought that she was Dan Kramer's wife and that he was in town shocked me. I guess I had been fooling myself by hoping he wouldn't show up, that this whole business was imaginary and it would never develop into the threat that Caroline and Pappy Jordan had indicated it would.

As I started to climb the stairs I glanced back at her. She sat motionless, a placid expression on her face, her hands clutching a reticule on her lap. She was waiting for someone, probably Kramer, waiting with a kind of monumental patience. She seemed completely oblivious to time passing and to her surroundings. I had the feeling that this was a situation she was used to and she was certain that sooner or later she would be taken to the next stop. In this case it would be Anchor.

I climbed the stairs to the second-story hall, but before I reached Caroline's room she opened the door and motioned for me to come into her room. She said, "I saw you cross the street to the hotel. I thought you were coming to see me." She smiled. "Or let's say I hoped you were."

I stepped into the room and she closed the door, then walked past me to the window. "Sit down, Sheriff," she said. "I've spent most of the day here at the window watching your town. It's been interesting, like seeing a small play with a few characters. I'm sure it would be more interesting if I knew all of the actors, their names and what they did for a living and who loves who and who hates someone else."

"It's all there," I said as I crossed the room to stand beside her. "I think you do know a good many of the actors. The plot has got more complicated in the last hour or two."

She glanced at me sharply as if trying to discover exactly what I meant. Her face showed no trace of a smile. It was, instead, very grim. I wondered if she was thinking that it was near the end of the third act, and the ending was not a pleasant one.

"Yes, I know some of them," she said. "My sister arrived shortly after you rode out of town with a man I presume was your prisoner, though I wondered why you weren't jailing him."

"He hadn't committed any crime," I said. "Not that I knew of anyway. I guess

155

that even making him leave town was more than I had a legal right to do."

"Who was he?"

"I don't know for sure," I said, "but after what you told me about Kramer and him bringing Buck Sharkey to Purgatory, I jumped to the conclusion that he was Sharkey."

She didn't say anything for a time. She was staring out of the window again. Finally she said, "The timing was right, but running him out of town did not solve your problem."

"I know that," I said, "but it gave me a little time. I want to talk to Kramer."

"You'll get your chance," she said. "He'll want to see you. He'll try to beat you down and scare the hell out of you." She glanced at me, wondering, I thought, just how much I would scare. She went on, "There is one thing I don't think I told you yesterday. It may not be important. The truth is I don't know all I should know. My sister didn't know every move Kramer was making, and I don't suppose she wrote all that she did know, but she wrote something about Kramer and the Purgatory banker having a working agreement, that the sheriff was an old man who wouldn't give Kramer any trouble."

She turned to me. "It's all different now, so Kramer is going to be jumpy, but I know him well enough to be sure that he will not leave any loopholes open that he can't close. You'll hear from him. If he finds that he can't intimidate you, he'll see that you're killed, too."

I stood motionless, staring down into the empty street. The harsh afternoon sunlight was almost blinding as it slanted down upon the dust strip from the west. The days were getting shorter, I thought irrelevantly. The sun would be setting before long.

Somehow I couldn't quite grasp what she had told me; I couldn't believe that Dan Kramer or any man would be as vicious or callous toward human life as she claimed he was. Then I realized that history was full of such men and human nature didn't change as much as we liked to believe.

I remember Caleb saying something like that. Man is inherently evil, he contended, and born in sin. I had to admit that some were. We just hadn't had any men like that in Turner County for a long time.

"Kramer and my sister came into the hotel," Caroline said after a long silence. "I guess they had dinner. I saw Kramer and Pappy Jordan go into the bank. Half an hour later or more Jordan left. He rode out of town a little after that, but Kramer is still over there in the bank."

She told me what I guessed had happened. That is, if I had been writing the play, I would have written it exactly as she said it had happened. There was one scene I still couldn't write, so I said, "Mark Vance told me you bought a shotgun. He owns the Mercantile and he was the man who sold it to you. Why do you need a shotgun?"

"You ought to know," she said tartly. "I told you I was going to kill Dan Kramer. I didn't bring a gun with me. I'm a good shot, so I could use a rifle, but I thought a shotgun would be more certain. I don't know how or when I'll get my chance, but I'll get it."

"My God!"

I stared at her and saw still another face. No smile, no plain run-of-the-mill grimness I had seen a few minutes ago, but one of vicious hatred. I didn't have the slightest doubt she would do exactly what she had said she was going to do if and when the right chance came along. In a small way, I think, I saw in her a trace of the same kind of callousness toward human life that apparently gripped Dan Kramer.

"I know what you're thinking," she said. "You don't believe a woman can feel the way I do about Dan Kramer. That's the way men are supposed to feel, not women. Well, I'm a woman, Sheriff, and believe me, that is the way I feel. Being a woman doesn't change anything. You can arrest me now or later, but I hope it will be later."

"You haven't done anything yet I can arrest you for," I said, "but if you do what you say you're going to, I will arrest you. You can count on it."

I moved to the door, and as I put a hand on the knob, she walked toward me.

"First, I want to save some lives here in Turner County," she said. "Second, I love my sister — although there have been times when I hated her, too — and I love her enough to free her from a marriage that is a catastrophe. I'll save her life by killing Kramer. I told you yesterday that he will murder her if I give him time to do it. Third, I want to pay him back for what he did to me. I have plenty of reasons to kill him, and I will never lose a second of sleep over it. Oh, and please don't tell my sister I'm here in Purgatory. I don't want her or Kramer to know. Not yet, anyway."

I left the room without another word,

leaving her standing there within three feet of the door. What can you say to a woman who tells you she is going to murder a man? I had never seen a woman like Caroline Dallas, and I never wanted to see another one.

Chapter XIV

The fat woman was still sitting in the lobby in exactly the position she had been in when I'd gone up to Caroline's room. On impulse I walked toward her, touching the brim of my hat as I said, "You're Mrs. Kramer, aren't you?"

She looked at me, but none of her body moved except her eyes. She said, "Yes. How did you know?"

I stood a few feet from her, thinking she would be a good-looking woman if she lost fifty pounds or more. I could see little resemblance to Caroline except for the auburn hair and blue eyes. Her face was empty of expression, and I had the feeling she didn't move a muscle except under duress.

"I had heard you and your husband would be in town," I said. "I want to see him when he comes in."

"You're the sheriff?"

"Yes ma'am. My name's Ed Logan. Tell your husband I'll be in my office in the jail building back of the courthouse."

"I thought the sheriff was an old man.

You seem very young."

"I guess I am," I said. "The other sheriff was killed. I've been appointed to serve out his term."

"I'll tell my husband," she said.

"Thank you," I said and left the lobby.

I could see little that was attractive about the woman, and as I walked to my office I wondered how two sisters could be so different. Caroline was vibrant and attractive and impelled by strong emotions. Mrs. Kramer seemed to be opposite in all respects, and if Dan Kramer was the kind of man Caroline claimed he was, I could believe what she said about him murdering his wife. Once he had completed his plans and all of the property and money was in his name, he would not be burdened by the blob of flesh that was his wife.

I had not gone through the sheriff's desk. I simply hadn't had time. It seemed to me that I had been on the run ever since I'd pinned on the star. I had time now while I waited for Kramer to show up, so I sat down in my swivel chair and opened one drawer after another. One was empty, one had a half-filled whiskey bottle, and the others held various kinds of paper, some legal documents that didn't mean a thing to me, but would after I'd been in office a while. In the right hand bottom drawer I hit what I was looking for: a stack of reward dodgers.

As I thumbed through the stack, I discovered that some were so old they were yellowed by age and were not of any value now. I examined the ones that appeared to be up-to-date. Most of them concerned men who were wanted in other parts of the country and probably would never come within five hundred miles of Turner County.

On the bottom of the pile was one that set me back in my chair. The picture was crude, but it was unquestionably the man I had escorted out of town. His name was Jud Hirsch. He was wanted in Las Animas County for defrauding a Trinidad business man out of ten thousand dollars.

He had a half dozen aliases. I was fascinated by his record. He had been an actor, touring the country with several player troupes, and had taken villain parts from Simon Legree on down the line. I thought he looked the part of a villain without putting on any makeup. Play-acting was one way to take advantage of his normal ugliness. On the other hand, I found it hard to believe that he could successfully impersonate a financial expert and defraud anyone, but then I suppose there are as many idiots who have money to invest as there are idiots who actually hold responsible jobs. I could imagine Simon Ross falling for a scheme that promised big returns. Trinidad probably had its share of men exactly like Simon Ross.

I looked up, suddenly aware that a man stood in the doorway. He would be Dan Kramer. I had more or less pictured him as a holy terror with horns and tails. He was anything but that. Handsome, tall, slender, he had the good shoulders and tapering body of a cowman, and although he wore a brown, broadcloth suit with a gold chain across his vest, he was obviously an outdoor man.

He was not, as far as I could tell, carrying a gun. He didn't speak for a time and neither did I. I didn't stand up and he made no effort to shake hands. He said in a voice that was indifferent, perhaps even hostile, "I'm Dan Kramer."

"I'm Ed Logan," I said.

Silence then, while we continued to size each other up. By this time he must have heard I was not the wet-behind-the-ears kid he might have judged me to be, and it was clear he was making a mental estimate of me. I had my mind made up about him, but if I hadn't heard what I had from both Caroline and Pappy Jordan, I'd have been taken in.

I had heard about men who simply overpowered people they met. I'm not sure how this comes about, but I suppose it's a combination of several qualities: looks, personality, bearing and the like. I knew that Judge Willoughby and Pappy Jordan had been men like that in their younger days. Even as old and mellowed as they were, I still felt some of that strange and mystical quality about them. Dan Kramer was that kind of man, now at the height of his powers. He knew that he had it and he used it in an overbearing and insulting way.

Kramer said bluntly, "My wife said you wanted to see me."

I nodded. "I've heard about you and what you plan to do. I don't like it worth a damn." I rose, deciding to make my offensive move right at the start, and motioned toward a chair. "Sit down. I want to tell you exactly where you stand."

He laughed. It was very unpleasant, a spine-chilling sound that affected me the way a piece of chalk sometimes grated on the blackboard. He said in a very abrasive tone, "I'd heard you were a snot-nosed kid who was too big for his pants. I aim to cut you down a few sizes. You can listen to where you stand."

I moved around the end of the desk, the blood pounding in my forehead. He had made up his mind he could simply roll over me and that this was the time to do it. I took a few seconds to control my fury. I knew that this was exactly the way he intended to affect me, and I had no intention of letting him take advantage of my temper.

"I'll listen if you'll stand and listen to me," I said. "I think I can be as insulting as you are."

"I'm not going to stand and listen to you," he said. "Not about anything. I'm fixing to tell you what you're going to do. You'll get on your horse and visit all the ranchers on the west side of the river. Tell them they're selling out to me. I'll pay more for their outfits than their property is worth. They are to be in the bank tomorrow afternoon from one to three. They'll be paid then and we'll make out the necessary papers."

"I'm not your errand boy," I said. "I won't tell them anything of the kind. What's more, they won't sell to you for any price."

"They will when they get my message," he said. "You'll be responsible for their deaths if you don't do what I told you to."

I started to say something, but before I could get a word out of my mouth, he did a very strange thing. He stepped into my office, closed the door, walked past me into the cells behind me and looked around. When he saw they were empty, he strode back across my office to the door, then turned to face me.

"I wanted to be damned sure that no one hears this but you, kid," he said. "I will deny every word of it if I'm ever in court, which I don't expect to be. A jury would believe an established rancher before they would their boy sheriff. I'm going to tell you what will happen. I will kill anyone who opposes me. I have a big deal ahead of me, too big for me to let anyone take it away from me.

"There is going to be a complete change in who runs this county." He paused to let his words soak in. "I have just met with Simon Ross and we have a working agreement. From now on he and I will run Turner County. He has the money. I have the power. Don't think you'll ever nail me for the killings because I'll be seen some place that's a long ways from where the shootings occur. To close the deal I have going for me, I have to own all the valley and I don't have much time. You're wrong about these men not selling to me. The first killing will soften them up. Or it may take two."

He turned to the door, put a hand on the knob and looking back over his shoulder, said, "One more thing, boy. Watch your step or I'll rub you out, too. You'd better change your mind about being my errand boy while you're still alive to do any changing."

"I won't," I shouted. "You'll be in court, all right, and I'll hang your hide. . . ."

I stopped. I didn't have anybody to talk to. Kramer was striding toward the courthouse and paying no attention whatever to what I was saying. I sat down behind my desk again, suddenly beginning to shake. If anyone had ever told me I would hear a man talk that way about murders he was going to pay for, I would have said it was crazy, that no human being would speak that easily and callously about murdering other men. He was as indifferent as if he had been talking about slaughtering a herd of steers.

Now I would believe every word Caroline had said about Dan Kramer: his raping her, murdering his wife, rubbing out his neighbors. All of it. He could charm a bird out of the sky or fire a bullet into a man's head with equal indifference.

I sat there quite a while thinking about it and wondering if I should take his message to the ranchers west of the North Fork. I doubted that I would save any lives. It was my guess that he was determined to commit at least one murder to soften them up. I had no way of guessing who the first one would be, or how much softening it would do, but I was certain of one thing. No one on the North Fork would sell now or even believe what I told them.

My thoughts turned from Kramer to the man named Jud Hirsch. There was nothing in his record to indicate he had ever been a gunslick or a paid killer. If he were Buck Sharkey or even if he had been suspected of being Sharkey, there would have been some mention of it on the reward notice. It did not even indicate he was dangerous. On the other hand, it was known that he had been an actor. Maybe, just maybe, he had been hired to play the part of Sharkey; it was a bluff all the way.

It seemed a crazy idea. No sane man would have any part of it. But Jud Hirsch might not be a very sane man. If he had been having trouble making a living as an actor or if he really was on the run from the crooked deal he'd pulled in Trinidad, he might have taken an assignment like this to hide out from the law and pick up a chunk of money to boot. Why? There seemed to be only one logical answer. He was a decoy for the real Sharkey.

There would not be much danger to Hirsch as long as he was protected by Kramer. If so, the real Sharkey had not showed up. Maybe he wouldn't. Maybe he'd stay out of town and not be seen by anyone, while Hirsch would be suspected of the killings. The trick, of course, was that we'd have a hard time convicting him.

It seemed complicated and farfetched, then I thought of Dan Kramer. In the few minutes I had faced him I had come to some definite conclusions about him. He was capable of any criminal act. He was mean. He was calculating. If Caroline had told the truth, he was also devious, the kind of man who would think up a complicated scheme like this, who would be ruthless in directing it but who would not pull any triggers himself.

I finally rose, aware that it was dusk and I hadn't eaten any supper. I'd get a drink in the hotel bar, then have one of Beulah's foot-long steaks, and go to bed. I'd sleep tonight, I told myself. I was tired; the sleepless hours of the previous night had caught up with me.

All I could do now was to wait for more of Kramer's plan to unravel before I could move to stop him. I was sure there would be one or more murders and I could do nothing to prevent them. Maybe, if I was lucky, I could nail Kramer before he killed off all the ranchers on the west side. I'd sure as hell try.

I left the office, wishing I had locked Hirsch up regardless of whether it was legal or not. When I reached the street, I heard a horse coming into town from the west. He was running, something few riders have their horses do in Turner County. We just don't have emergencies requiring that kind of speed from a horse. A moment later I made out the horse and rider in the dim light and waited along the street until he reached me, an uneasy feeling crawling into my belly.

When the rider saw me, he reined up. It was Bud Campbell. I think I knew what had happened before he opened his mouth. He leaned down, and even as thin as the light was, sensed the grief that twisted his face.

"Gramp was shot and killed about half

an hour ago," he yelled at me. "I'm gonna get the preacher and Doc Wardell."

He cracked steel to his horse and thundered on down Main Street. I stood motionless, staring after him in the twilight, my uneasiness turning into an aching sickness. So it had started!

Chapter XV

I ran to the livery stable and called to Hubey, "Harness up Doc's mare and hitch her to his buggy."

I saddled Alexander and led him into the street, then waited until Doc came striding along the boardwalk, not even pausing when he passed me. I said, "I told Hubey to harness up for you." He disappeared into the stable. A few minutes later Bud returned. I stepped into the saddle and rode out of town with him. We didn't say anything for a long time. Presently Doc caught us, laying his whip across his mare's back, something he rarely did. Caleb Watts was in the seat beside him.

We pulled off the road and let them pass. I wasn't in a hurry to reach the Campbell place. I guess Bud wasn't either. He always had been a great one to talk whether he had much to say or not, but he wasn't talking tonight.

We reached the lane that led to the Campbell ranch before I asked, "How did it happen, Bud?"

He didn't answer until we reined up in

front of the house. I stepped down and tied at the hitch rail beside Doc's mare. Bud stayed in the saddle looking down at me. The last of the red glow in the west had died now and there was no moon. Bud's face was a pale blob in the almost total darkness. Several times on the way here I had heard a muffled sob break out of him. When we were kids I would always cry before Bud did, but tonight he had more than he could manage.

"I don't know, Ed," he said, his voice so low I barely heard what he said. "It just happened. We were going to the house for supper and were about halfway there when I heard a rifle shot. I didn't realize what had happened until I'd gone about a dozen steps. I looked back and Gramp was on the ground. I ran back to him. He was dead. He must have died on his feet."

"You know where the shot came from?"

"No. I didn't even see any smoke." He paused, trying to hold back the tears. Then he went on. "The shot wasn't fired from right close, but it wasn't far off, neither. I guess I didn't pay much attention. I'd been thinking about what you said when you were out here. I'd tried to tell Gramp to stay inside, but you know how stubborn he is." He stopped, then added, "I mean was."

Bud rode off toward the corral and I went into the house. The front room was empty, but the door into the bedroom was open. When I looked in, I had the impression the room was jammed with people. The body was on the bed. Mrs. Campbell was sitting beside it holding the dead man's hand.

Ma was bending over the old woman trying to get her to come into the front room, but Mrs. Campbell kept shaking her head. Caleb was standing behind Ma. He was a good minister and an efficient man, but at the moment he didn't seem to know what to do. I stopped in the doorway and decided there was no sense in me going into the bedroom. One more person would just add to the crowd. Doc Wardell was standing at the foot of the bed, scowling. When he saw me, he moved to me and we stepped back into the front room.

"Dunno why Bud wanted me to come out here," Doc said. "The old man was dead the instant the slug hit him. Dead center. Whoever fired that shot was a hell of a good marksman." He scratched his chin. "You gonna find out who done it?"

"I aim to," I said. "I've got a hunch who it was."

The scowl left his face. "Who?"

"The man I ran out of town this afternoon," I said. "I knew he was no damn good, but he hadn't committed any crime I could hold him for, so I took the law into my own hands and saw that he got as far as the Narrows. I thought he'd keep going, but now I'm guessing he circled back into the valley and dry gulched the old man."

"Why?"

"Somebody must have paid him to kill Campbell," I said. "The man was a stranger. He had no reason to do it."

"Who paid him?"

I couldn't tell Doc what I knew and what I suspected. I just didn't know enough and he wouldn't believe my guesses, so I said, "That's what I've got to find out."

Doc shrugged. "I hope you do, son. I hope you do."

"It might have been Simon Ross," I said.

Doc had started toward the front door, but what I said brought him around in a hurry. "Now that is the damnedest accusation I ever heard in my born days. You loco?"

"I reckon I am," I said. "I guess nobody would ever suspect a banker of doing anything wrong."

"Whoa now," Doc said. "I wouldn't say that. Have you got any evidence?"

"Not a bit," I said. "It was just a hunch, but something's wrong with Ross. No sane man would have supported Max Moran for the sheriff's job and worked so hard to get me to quit. He didn't give any reason for wanting me out."

Doc scratched his chin again, a characteristic gesture when he was annoyed and worried to boot. He said, "It is a mite peculiar at that, but you'd better be careful who you say that to." He started for the door once more, and when he reached it, he said, "I'm going back to town. Tell Bud to bring the preacher back to town when he wants to come. Oh, your Pa's gone to tell the neighbors."

I nodded, and he went on through the door and down the path to his buggy. I'd sure been right about one thing, I thought. Gramp Campbell would be alive if he'd believed me and stayed in the house. I had a notion to wait and tell Pa again that he had to stay inside, but I knew he wouldn't. Anyhow, I needed to get back and go to bed. I had plenty to do in the morning.

When I returned to the bedroom, I saw that Ma had moved away from Mrs. Campbell and Caleb was sitting beside her talking in a low voice. He was doing what he should do and he was good at it when given the opportunity. Ma saw me and came toward me, dabbing at her eyes.

"I don't think she's hearing a thing any of us say," Ma said, her face marked by an expression of sheer despair. "Doc says she's in shock. I want to get her to bed, but she just sits there and doesn't say a thing."

"Pa's gone to tell the neighbors," I said. "You'll have help soon."

She nodded absentmindedly, her mind still on Mrs. Campbell. "I guess we'll just have to pick her up and carry her into the other bedroom. I think she's practically unconscious."

"It'll be Pa tomorrow if he doesn't stay under cover," I said, "but I don't know how to make him do it."

Ma grabbed my arms, her face turning pale. "Why? Why, Ed? Pa never did any harm to anyone!"

"Of course not," I said, "but that's got nothing to do with it. The man who bought Pappy Jordan out wants the whole valley and he won't stop at murder or anything else to get it. I'd arrest him tonight if I had any solid evidence. I'm sure he's the one behind this murder."

Ma turned away from me and walked to the door and looked out into the darkness. She said in a tone so low I barely heard her, "What will we do, Ed?"

"I dunno," I said. "Pa knows for sure that what I told him last night is true, but that's not going to keep him inside the house."

"I could do the chores," Ma said. "The murderer wouldn't shoot a woman."

"I can't see Pa letting you do that," I said.

"Oh, I know," she said. "Why do men have to be that way when it's a matter of life and death?"

"It's the way we are," I said. "I can understand the way Pa feels. I guess I'd do the same if I was in his boots. But I can't understand how a man like Dan Kramer can hire someone to kill men in cold blood. He told me that was what he would do if people didn't sell to him."

"Isn't that enough to arrest him for?"

I shook my head. "It's only my word against his. He was mighty careful to see that no one overheard him say it. He told me he'd deny it in court and that the jury would believe him instead of a kid sheriff. I expect he's right."

Ma took a long, sighing breath. "It's downright crazy, isn't it, Ed? We've always had to work hard, but we've been willing to do that, and we've made a living. I think

179

we've been happier than most married couples, though your Pa is an uncommonly stubborn man at times. We've got along pretty well. Everything's been peaceful except for Pa's tiff with Simon Ross. Now this. It just isn't right."

"No it's not for a fact," I said.

Right then I felt like riding out to Anchor and shooting Dan Kramer down like the mad dog he was. I think I might have done exactly that if I hadn't pinned on the star, but now I wasn't just the son of a rancher or a private citizen. I was something special. I was all the law there was in Turner County.

Caleb and Mrs. Campbell came out of the bedroom, Caleb's arm around the old woman's waist. She was walking, but she was swaying back and forth like a willow in a high wind. Every step was an effort. Her eyes were glassy. I didn't think she knew where she was or what she was doing. Ma hurried to them and together with Caleb helped Mrs. Campbell across the front room and into the kitchen. Bud's room was next to the kitchen and they put her to bed there.

"I'm going to town, Ma," I called.

She was so concerned about Mrs. Campbell that I don't believe she heard me, but she'd know where I'd gone. Other neighbors would be here in a few minutes and I certainly wasn't needed. When I left the house, I found Bud in front standing beside Alexander.

"Gramma all right?" Bud asked.

"She's taking it pretty hard," I said. "Bud, I may need a good man with a gun before this is over. How'd you like to serve as my deputy?"

I couldn't see him very well, but he stood beside me, motionless as near as I could tell. He didn't say a word for quite a while. As long as I had known Bud, I had never doubted his courage, but I did now when he said, "I guess I'd better not, Ed. I ought to stay here."

"All right," I said, and untied Alexander.

I mounted and headed for town, anger stirring in me. There was no one else in Turner County I could ask for help until it came down to a final crunch. I was sure that Pa or some of the other ranchers would do their best for me if they had to and there were a few townsmen like Mark Vance who would help, but they were older men with families and I didn't want to ask them to risk their lives in a situation like this. Maybe I would later, but I had to know more than I did now.

One thing I wasn't sure about. Would the Anchor crew back Kramer? I didn't think so, but Kramer was their boss now and I couldn't be sure. If I had to go to Anchor to arrest Kramer and the crew did back him up, I'd be in hell of a tight spot.

Hubey wasn't in a sight when I rode into the livery stable. He'd probably gone to bed and there was no reason for me to wake him up. His boss practically left him in charge of the stable, a big job for a kid as young as Hubey. His boss was more interested in trading horses and riding to neighboring towns like Gunnison and Montrose than he was in renting horses and cleaning up horse manure. Hubey needed the money because he supported his mother and I think he was paid pretty well. He liked his job, so I was sure he was satisfied.

I pulled gear from Alexander and turned him into the corral behind the stable. I walked through the darkness to my house, but I hadn't gone far before I stopped and stared at it in sheer amazement.

There was a light in the front room and the door was wide open. For a moment I stood there, trying to figure out who would be paying me a visit, but I didn't have a guess. It wouldn't be Dan Kramer. Not the man who called himself Buck Smith, either. They wouldn't light a lamp to announce their presence.

I drew my gun and eased toward the front door. I was sure that whoever was here was a friend, but I wasn't of mind to take any chances.

Chapter XVI

I felt ridiculous, holding my gun in my right hand as I eased across the porch and slid through the front door. No one was in sight. I paused, wondering if by some crazy streak of absentmindedness I had lit the lamp and left it burning. I dismissed the idea immediately.

Still holding the gun in my hand, I picked up the lamp with my left hand and carried it into the kitchen. I even looked in the pantry, then crossed to the bedroom. I stopped in the doorway, my heart skipping a beat. A woman was asleep in my bed. She was lying on her side, her back to me, her skirt pulled up almost to her waist so that I found myself looking at most of her shapely right leg.

I put the lamp on the bureau and turned the woman over. Before I saw her face, I was sure it was Caroline Dallas. Now that she was on her back, I saw I had been right. I sat down on the edge of the bed and looked at her. She kept on sleeping after I turned her over.

During the time I had spent with Caroline Dallas, I had seen a variety of expressions on her face. Now it was very peaceful, almost the face of a young and innocent girl, exactly opposite to the vindictive hatred I had seen when she'd said frankly that she was going to kill Dan Kramer.

I reached over and shook her. Her eyes opened and shut and opened again, but it was a full minute before she became aware of where she was and who I was. She rubbed her eyes and smiled as she murmured, "Oh, there you are." The hem of her skirt was still up almost to her waist, but it didn't bother her. The smile faded and she demanded, "Where the hell have you been? I've been waiting a long time for you."

"It isn't any of your business where I've been," I sad angrily. "Would you mind telling me exactly what you're doing here."

"Waiting to see you," she snapped. "What do you think?"

"I don't know what to think," I said, "but I'll tell you one thing. I'm not used to coming home and finding a woman in my bed."

She giggled. "I'm not in your bed. I'm on it. There is a difference. I just plain got tired of waiting for you. I was sleepy, so came in here and laid down."

"You can tell me what you want to tell me," I said, "then get the hell out of here and sleep in your own bed. I'm too tired to spend the rest of the night arguing with you."

She pursed out her lips and stared at me thoughtfully. "Oh, I don't know about that. You might find out you're not as tired as you think." She patted the bed at her side. "Lie down here and I'll tell you why I'm here."

"Get out of here," I said and stood up. "I don't think you had anything to tell me."

She smiled again, a kind of superior smile as if telling me I didn't know what I really wanted or what I should do. I felt as if I was ten years old and she was a very experienced woman who had been everywhere and had done everything.

"Oh yes, I have something to tell you," she said.

She sat up on the bed and rubbed her eyes. "I was sleeping so well. You're a brute for waking me up. You're not the only one who's tired. I got to thinking last night about my sister and Kramer and why I was here. It's something you can't really understand, Sheriff. I'm not sure I understand it myself, but I've been through too much and hated Dan Kramer too long to go back and not do what I came here to do."

I picked up the lamp and carried it into the front room, jerking my head at her. "Come on out here. We'll talk about two minutes and then you get out of here."

She followed, laughing softly. "You're a blind man, Sheriff. I could be very amusing, you know, but I guess you're above temptation."

I set the lamp on the stand. "All right," I said. "What do you want to tell me?"

"Why don't you start a fire and make some coffee," she said. "It would clear your head."

"Oh no," I said. "My head's clear enough. What do you want to say?"

"For one thing," she said slowly as if she knew she was making me angry by dragging it out, "you have a nice-looking girl."

"What do you know about her?" I demanded.

"Oh, quite a bit," she said. "Of course I'm reading between the lines." She sat down in a rocking chair and crossed her legs. "She was here this evening. We had a little argument. I think she was put out at finding me here. She thought she could outwait me, but I told her she couldn't, so she finally went home."

I stared at Caroline, hating her. I had enough worries about Sharon without having the woman make things worse. I said, "By God, if you lied to her and made her think there was anything between us, I'll break your neck."

"No you won't," she said. "You need me. Anyhow, I didn't lie to her. I don't know what she thought, but it wasn't good. I told her I had business with you and I was going to wait until you got back."

"Did she say what she wanted with me?"

"No, but she said something about fixing a date. She didn't tell me what kind of a date she was talking about."

I hadn't seen Sharon all day and she must have expected me to call. Apparently she had made up her mind about when she'd marry me and set a date. At least I could hope it was that way. On the other hand, she might be so mad after finding Caroline Dallas here that she decided not to marry me at all.

"I still don't know why you're here," I said.

She shrugged her shoulders as if admitting she had played cat and mouse with me long enough. She said, "I wanted to know if you saw Kramer today."

"I sure did," I said. "He told me enough to confirm everything that you said about him. He's the biggest bastard I ever ran into. I think he is capable of murdering your sister like you said he would."

"He is and he will," she said, "if I let him." She paused, her face again twisted by the hatred that was scarring her soul. "I guess you're convinced now that I have reason to kill him."

"He needs killing and that's a fact," I said. "He started his killing tonight."

I told her about Gramp Campbell. She asked, "You have any idea who pulled the trigger?"

"It might have been the fellow I kicked out of town today," I said. "I didn't think he could get back this soon and find a gun, but maybe he did. I wanted to lock him up but he hadn't done anything."

"You know his name?"

"He said it was Buck Smith," I answered, "but I found a reward dodger with a picture on it that sure looks like him. It said he was Jud Hirsch."

"I've heard of him," she said. "He defrauded a Trinidad man out of some money." She shook her head. "I saw him this afternoon when he walked up the street carrying his two guns. You know,

189

Sheriff, he didn't have any reputation around Trinidad as a gunman, but he looked like he would fill the bill. I suppose he wanted you to think he was Buck Sharkey, so he called himself Buck Smith."

"That's my guess," I said. "He's an actor. He could play any part he wanted."

She shook her head. "You're wrong about that, Sheriff. There are some roles that even an actor can't play in real life. Taking the part of a gunman is one. Not successfully anyway."

"Maybe," I said, irritated by her implication that I had a lot to learn. I knew I did, but I didn't think she knew everything. "I've got to find some evidence that ties Kramer in with the murder. Right now I don't have anything."

"I think it's all going to come out to-morrow," she said. "That's really why I came over here tonight. I'm not sure if I told you this, but I wanted to remind you. Kramer is in a terrible hurry. Like I said, my sister didn't write everything to me. She was so worked up that some of what she wrote was garbled, but I know that Kramer is caught in a time squeeze. To make this big deal he has pending, he's got to get these other ranches lined up in a hurry. That's why he had the man killed

190

today. He figures this will stampede every-body into selling."

"It won't," I said. "He ordered me to see all of the west side ranchers and tell them what their choice was. I told him I wasn't his errand boy. How were they supposed to know he wants to buy them out?"

"Didn't you see the last copy of the *Puragatory Press*?

"No. It hadn't come when I left home," I said. "We should have had it but I guess our copy was mixed up in the mail."

"Kramer had a big ad on the front page," she said. "It tells them to be in town to-morrow and see him in the bank. He promised to pay a handsome figure for any and all ranches west of the river."

"No threats?"

"No," she answered. "Not directly any-how, but they'll get the point. If they don't show up at the bank tomorrow, he'll prob-ably see them personally to give them a nudge. There's another thing. I warned you about it, but I don't think you took it seriously. Kramer's plans were upset when the old sheriff died and a young buck like you got appointed. He'll rub you out just to get you out of his way."

"I can't sit around waiting for that to happen," I said.

"Well, whatever you do, you'd better do in a hurry," she said. "His old crew will show up before long and they're a bunch of hard cases. When they get here, Kramer will really rule the valley."

"Why aren't they here now?" I asked.

"I'm guessing they're not very far away," she answered. "He probably didn't bring them because he had promised Jordan to keep the old crew. He didn't want Jordan backing out of the deal, but now it's made and he can fire the old crew. You'll see."

"All right, I'll watch out," I said, suddenly so tired I felt as if I didn't give a damn about anything. "Get out of here so I can go to bed."

She walked to the door, put a hand on the knob and looked back at me, the tantalizing smile on her lips again. "Sure you won't regret your decision as soon as I'm out of the door? I can stay, you know. Nobody's waiting for me in my room."

I started toward her, my fists clenched. I'd had all of her teasing I was going to. I don't know what I would have done if she'd stayed, but she opened the door and slipped out and shut the door quickly. Her seductive laugh still rang in my ears. I tried to put both her and Sharon out of my mind, along with the other problems that seemed to have multiplied a dozen times in the last few hours. But the wheels kept turning in my head, with the result that I slept little more than I had the previous night.

The Third Day

Chapter XVII

In spite of my effort not to think of what was happening, my mind kept returning to it. I guess I spent most of the night sorting out what had to be done the next day, not knowing, of course, exactly what Kramer would do or when he would do it.

The first thing I would do in the morning would be to ride out along the river to where I thought the dry gulcher had hidden when he'd shot Gramp Campbell and try to pick up any sign I could. The chances were I wouldn't find anything, but even the smartest man can make mistakes. I thought I might find something. A long chance, but it seemed to me it was worth the trouble.

The second thing I would do would be to go to the bank. If there was a working agreement between Kramer and Simon Ross, I wanted to know what it was. I also wanted to know why Ross had backed Max Moran and had been so determined to keep me from getting the star.

I had thought about this a good deal ever since Ross had made it clear that he would do his best to move me out of the sheriff's office. The banker was no fool, so he had to have a reason for supporting a man that everyone knew was incompetent, lazy and dishonest.

I don't know how much I slept, but suddenly I woke with prickles racing down my spine. Someone was in my bedroom. I eased a few inches toward the stand beside the head of the bed where I had left my gun. I probably wouldn't have had time to get hold of it if the intruder aimed to kill me, but I couldn't think of anything else to do. The next thing I knew the foot of the bed sagged as someone sat down.

"You awake, Ed?"

It was Sharon's voice. I relaxed, taking a deep breath and feeling like an idiot. I wanted to shake her. My voice sounded weak to my ears when I asked, "What in the hell are you doing here?"

"I came to see if you had that bitch in bed with you," she said.

I was too groggy to think whom she meant for a moment, then I remembered that Caroline had said Sharon had been here. When I remembered, I was furious. I started to throw off the covers and stand up, then remembered I wasn't wearing anything but my drawers.

"Get out of here and let me dress," I snapped. "This is the damnedest, stupidest thing you have ever done in your life. I ought to paddle you."

"I wish you would," she said. "It would show you cared."

"Cared?" I yelled. "Of course I care. I've cared for a long time, but what you're doing proves you don't trust me."

She rose and moved to the head of the bed. "I trust you," she said in a voice that was low and halting. "I don't trust that woman. She told me she was going to sleep until you got here. That meant she'd be in your bed. I don't blame a man when a woman as attractive as that tart throws herself at you."

"Get out of here," I said. "I won't be responsible for what I do to you if you don't go home."

"I'm not ready to go home," she said. "Not yet."

She drew back the covers far enough to slide in beside me. "Sharon, for God's sake," I groaned, "what are you trying to do to me."

She cuddled against me and, putting her hand on my head, turned it so I faced her. Then she kissed me. She had always been a great kisser, but this kiss was different. It was lingering, it was demanding. Suddenly her girlhood was a thing of the past. She was a woman making a woman's demands. It seemed as if she had awakened and found herself in a world of passionate love she had not known before.

When she finally drew back, she whispered, "How was that, darling?"

"If you're trying to seduce me, you've just about done the job," I said. "Now will you go home?"

"No," she whispered. "If I have about succeeded, then let's get at it."

I shoved her away from me and got out on the opposite side of the bed. I walked around the foot and started to dress, then I heard her crying. "Now what?" I demanded.

"What do you think?" she demanded. "If that woman had done what I've done, you wouldn't tell her to go home?"

"I did last night," I said. "I shoved her out of the front door."

She sniffed. "That's what she deserved. But she's so pretty, I didn't think you could do that."

"She's not as pretty as you are," I said. "If you're going to stay here, you might as well get up and make yourself useful, like cooking breakfast."

I left the bedroom and, going into the kitchen lit a lamp. The dawn light was still too thin to work by. Sharon followed me into the kitchen, dabbing at her tears. "I guess you don't think I can cook," she said. "I'll show you." She sniffled, then added, "I guess you think more of your belly than you do of . . . of other things."

I built a fire, and when I had it going, I said, "No. It's just that there's a lot going on that you don't know about. Gramp Campbell was murdered late yesterday. I've got to find the killer and bring him in. I may get killed. The one thing I won't do is to leave you with a baby in you and nobody to marry you. I wouldn't rest in hell if I did that."

She sat down, her face turning pale. "I . . . I didn't know," she said. "All I could think of was that awful woman. She said she was going to stay here until you got back and I might as well go home. She said she could outwait me so I left, but I couldn't sleep. I tried to read and I couldn't do that, either. Finally I woke Mamma up and told her what had happened. She said to go to you. She said I could show you I loved you as much as the other woman did. She said a lot of girls did it before they were married, so I came here."

I put the coffee pot on and got out the eggs and bacon I had brought from the store. There wasn't anything else to eat, so it would have to do. I didn't want to wait until Sharon mixed up a batch of biscuits. I turned to her and lifted her to her feet. I was shocked by what her mother had said, but I suppose I shouldn't have been. I had heard stories about women who took that way of getting a husband, but in my case it wasn't necessary. I had wanted to marry her any day she said.

"You've showed me," I said. "Now just what did you want to see me about last night?"

"I wanted to tell you I'd made up my mind and set a date," she said. "I'll marry you today or tomorrow or the day after tomorrow. I don't know why I played hard to get when you asked me to set a date. I want to marry you more than anything in the world and I always have."

I kissed her and said, "It was just the woman in you. They just naturally get perverse sometimes."

"I suppose you're an expert on women," she said.

"No, but I know that much," I said. "We'll set tomorrow. I'm just not sure what will happen today. I'll tell you all about it when it's over. Now you fry the bacon and eggs while I shave."

By the time we had finished eating, it was full daylight. I rose and blew out the lamp. I said, "I've got to saddle Alexander and start hunting."

"I'll clean up the dishes," she said.

She rose and we faced each other, but she was staring at the floor, not at me when she whispered, "I suppose you won't have any respect for me now. I've heard that's what happens when a woman is too easy. I'm ashamed, Ed."

I sighed. "Don't be," I said, thinking that being married to Sharon was not going to be easy. "I haven't lost any respect for you. The date is tomorrow. Why don't you go see Caleb this morning and find out if he's free to tie the knot tomorrow?"

I went into the bedroom and buckled my gun belt around me, then returned to the front room. Taking my hat off a peg near the door, I put it on my head. Sharon was still standing in the doorway between the kitchen and the bedroom.

As I put my hand on the knob to turn it, she said, "I do trust you, Ed. I'll always trust you."

For a moment we stood facing each other, Sharon looking at me as if she wanted to say something more, and I was thinking I ought to say something more, but I didn't know what it should be.

"I like this house," she said. "It will be a good home for us."

"I'm glad you like it," I said.

We were silent again for what seemed a long time although I know it was only a few seconds. I didn't want to leave her like this, but I didn't know what to do. It seemed to me we had said all there was to say.

"You come back to me," she burst out. "I'm sorry you were appointed sheriff."

"I'll be back," I promised. I opened the door and left the house.

The sun was up, but the night chill was still in the air and would be for another hour or more. I wished I had brought my coat from home, but it had been Indian summer for so long that I guess I was lulled into thinking it would last forever. Clouds were hanging down over the peaks, and though the sky was clear overhead, I guessed we'd have snow by tonight.

Hubey was around when I reached the livery stable, so I watered Alexander and saddled him, then mounted and rode out of town, heading downriver and keeping on the east side. The killer had probably stayed east of the river.

If I didn't bring the dry gulcher in soon, there would be another killing. I was certain that not all the ranchers would show up at the bank this afternoon, and the ones who did were not likely to sell. If they weren't panicked as Kramer expected them to be, the second shooting was inevitable.

I couldn't bring myself to think who the next victim would be. I tried to block it out of my thoughts, but as I rode, the tension built up in me, and the more certain I became that it would be my father.

Chapter XVIII

I had no way of knowing exactly where the killer had waited, but I guessed that he must have crossed the river to the west side and hidden among the willows until he got the shot he wanted. The place where he'd hidden must have been as close to the Campbell ranch as possible, but the willows grew thicker in some areas than others, so he might not have found a satisfactory hiding place as close to the Campbell buildings as I was thinking.

All I could do was to start looking. By the time I dismounted and tied Alexander, the sun was above the rim to the east, so the light was strong enough for me to see tracks or any other sign the killer had left.

I walked along the edge of the willows until I had gone past the point where I thought the assassin would have hidden. The ground was hard, and some of Pappy Jordan's horses had been pastured in this field, so there was a multitude of tracks.

I pushed through the edge of the willows to the bank and began walking along it, paralleling the route I had just taken.

Within fifty yards I found what I was looking for, a pile of horse manure and tracks in the soft earth next to the water where a horse had been tied. From the signs that had accumulated, I judged that the horse had been here quite a while.

I waded the river, which at this point ran swiftly across a gravel bed. It was shallow, not more than three or four inches. Here there was a gap in the willows on the west side, and when I had climbed the bank I found myself in the open. The Campbell buildings were directly in front of me. The killer, not wanting to take a chance on being seen, had probably not shown himself here, so I slid back to the mud along the edge of the water and moved upstream.

My guess had been right. The dry gulcher had moved upstream. I hadn't gone more than fifty feet until I found the place where he had scrambled up the steep bank. I found two distinct boot tracks in the soft earth. I studied them for several minutes, knowing that I'd probably never have a chance to fit the killer's boot into the tracks, but I did note several facts that might prove to be of value.

The boots were new or had recently been resoled. It was my guess that the boots were new. A man who followed the profession this man did would be well paid and it struck me that he wouldn't bother with having new heels and soles put on old boots. The man had big feet, bigger than mine by a couple of sizes, and he was a fairly heavy man judging by the depth of the tracks.

I pulled myself up the bank and saw where the killer had crawled through the willows to the west fringe. Here he had waited. I found burned matches but no cigarette stubs or cigar stubs, so he must be a pipe smoker,

From the way the grass had been pressed down, it appeared he had been lying on his belly for some time. The willows thinned out here so he had a clear shot at the Campbell yard. I spent several minutes feeling around in the grass and finally found a .30-.30 shell. I stuck it in my pocket, but I knew damn well it didn't mean a thing. I suppose there were more than a hundred .30-.30s in Turner County.

I apparently had found all that there was to find. I waded back across the stream and untied Alexander. I mounted, but I didn't move for several minutes. I stared at the Anchor buildings on the bench above the river, wondering if the killer was there. I mentally ran over what I had learned about the man: a pipe smoker, owned a .30-.30, probably had new boots, and was bigger than average. It added up to something, but not enough to convict a man of murder.

I had not forgotten Jud Hirsch. If he was the killer, he'd gotten hold of a rifle somewhere. Anchor would be the logical place to get one, unless he'd hidden one out or had met up with friends after he'd left me. I discarded both of these possibilities and decided that the chances were he would have returned to Anchor for supper after the killing and had likely stayed the night. As early as it was, I figured he more than likely was still there.

If Kramer had planned another killing today, Hirsch would certainly be around someplace. I knew one thing regardless of evidence or legal right. I'd jail him if I caught him again. I didn't know how long I could hold him, probably only until Judge Willoughby got back, but by that time I'd surely have enough evidence to hold the man or discharge him.

The only thing I could do now was to see if Hirsch was at Anchor. I'd take him even if it meant a showdown with Kramer. Maybe it was time for a showdown. I reined Alexander around and put him up the steep slope to the western edge of the bench.

My self-confidence had grown, perhaps foolishly, from the time I'd pinned the star on, until now. I thought I could take Kramer and Hirsch too if it came to that. I couldn't, even in my wildest fantasy, handle the Anchor crew.

I had known the Anchor foreman, Lars Larson, since I'd been a boy. He was a good cowman and Pa always said that he had more to do with keeping Anchor solvent than Pappy Jordan had. Larson was a tough man. I had been with him on several drives to the railroad at Gunnison, and I knew exactly how tough he could be.

Larson was also an honest man, and I had a hunch he wasn't going to get along with Dan Kramer. By the time I reached the bench, I had convinced myself that Larson would stay out of any fracas I had with Kramer. He might even support me. I knew that the crew would follow the foreman's lead.

The bench leveled off and the Anchor buildings lay directly in front of me: a sprawling barn, a maze of corrals, and a two-story ranch house that Pappy Jordan had built for his wife years ago. It was by far the biggest, best and most ornate ranch house in the county.

Several men were standing in front of a corral gate as I rode up, Larson among them. I knew most of the others, men who had been with Jordan for years, but Jud Hirsh was not with them. Neither was Kramer.

"You're out a mite early, ain't you, Sheriff?" Larson asked.

"It's no time to sleep in," I said.

"Get down and rest your saddle," Larson said. "Have breakfast?"

I nodded and dismounted, my gaze turning to the ranch house where Mrs. Kramer was sitting on the porch in a rocking chair. I had seen Mrs. Jordan sit in the same chair a dozen times and it didn't seem right for another woman to be there. I moved away from Alexander so that I had a clear view of the house and the bunkhouse. I had been so sure that Hirsch would be here that I had expected him to be with the crew.

"I'm looking for a stranger," I said. "A big man. Ugly as sin. Got a scar. . . ."

"He's here," Larson said. "He's in the bunkhouse with Kramer. You want him?"

The other men had shifted around uneasily as if wishing they were somewhere else, but Larson, in his slow, steady way, was just as solid as he ever was. My hope was rekindled that if I was cornered, he'd back my play.

"I want him, all right," I said. "I'm taking him in for Gramp Campbell's murder."

That startled them. Even Larson was surprised. He asked, "Ed, have you got the deadwood on him, or is it just your guess he done it?"

"I don't have the evidence now," I said, "but I'll get it."

"This ain't gonna be easy for you," Larson said. "Seems that this fellow and Kramer used to know each other. He rode in yesterday, mad as hell, and said you'd run him out of town. He wanted a place to stay, so Kramer took him in. He slept in the bunkhouse last night. Surly bastard. Didn't talk much."

"I'll go get him," I said.

"Now just hold on a minute," Larson said, moving away from the others, his bronze face showing no concern than I had ever seen in it. "You're young and inexperienced for this job. I don't want to see you bite no more than you can chew."

"Maybe that's what I'm doing," I said, "but the only way I'm going to get the truth is to take this man in and question him. I don't know how much Kramer has said to you or what you think of him, but he's the man behind Campbell's murder. Sooner or later I'm taking him in, too."

Larson glanced at his crew, then at me, and back at them, all the time chewing on his lower lip, his concern growing.

"I told you, Lars," one of the men said. "This Kramer gent is no damn good."

He was Sandy McGraw, a dried-up little Scot who had been with Jordan almost as long as Larson had. He was as feisty as a terrier pup, always on the prod, and I guessed he was the one man in the crew who might back me up, but knew it still depended on what Larson did.

"Shut up, Sandy," Larson said angrily. "We don't know much about Kramer, Ed, but I can't swallow what you're saying. I think you're like most kids. You're going off half-cocked."

That made me sore. I had expected to be called a kid when I'd pinned on the star, but I didn't feel like a kid. I'd lived about ten years in the last three days. I said hotly, "I'm not a kid, Lars. I saw Gramp Campbell's body last night after he'd been shot. I found the place where the killer had hidden in the brush. I've got enough evidence on Kramer to hang him ten times. Trouble is, it's not the kind of evidence I can use in court, but I'll get it. Now I'm going after Scarface. Kramer can wait. He won't go anywhere."

Larson grabbed my arm. "Slow down," he said irritably. "I guess we all feel like Sandy, but we don't know for sure yet. If we're gonna work for him, we owe him something. We just don't know yet, so we're waiting until we have something we can make up our minds on. I'm not gonna condemn a man on your say-so."

"I'm not asking you to," I said, "but I am surprised that you think you're working for him."

I wasn't playing this quite straight, but I knew that if Kramer and Hirsch came out of the bunkhouse together, I was in trouble. I had told myself a few minutes ago that I could handle 'em, but now that I was facing the job, I was scared. I wasn't going to back off, but I knew I had to have some help if I lived long enough to take Hirsch to town.

Larson looked at me questioningly. Sandy McGraw said, "Lay it on the table, Ed."

"All right," I said, "but I've got a question first. Has Kramer told you he was keeping you on?"

"No, he hasn't said anything," Larson

answered. "That's what we're waiting to hear, but just before he left Pappy told us he had made Kramer promise to keep us on. He said he wouldn't have sold out under any other conditions. Most of us aren't as young as we used to be and he said he didn't want to leave us up the creek."

"Pappy would do that," I said. "I talked to him yesterday morning. He was worrying about it just before he left town. He'd heard some things about Kramer that he didn't like."

"Like what?" Larson demanded. When I hesitated, not sure how much I should tell him, he added, "You're bulling us, ain't you, Ed? You're playing this tough and you expect us to give you a hand?"

"I'm not hankering to die this morning, Lars," I said, "so I'd appreciate any help I can get, but I don't expect any of you to serve as deputies or to fight for me. All I want is a chance to get Scarface off Anchor so I can take him to town."

"Fair enough," McGraw said.

"Damn it, Sandy, stay out of this," Larson said angrily. "Ed, I'm waiting to hear what it was that Pappy heard."

"I got it straight," I said, "that Kramer is into a big business deal that requires the whole valley, so he's buying out all the landholders on the west side. He aims to kill enough to panic the rest. Gramp Campbell was the first to go just to show the others what will happen if they don't sell."

"Oh hell," Larson exploded. "This ain't the seventies. Nobody ignores the law like that these days."

"I dunno about that," McGraw said. "There was an ad in the *Press* for 'em to meet with Kramer at the bank. You saw it, Lars."

"You took a dislike to Kramer the minute you seen him," Larson snapped. "You've been talking him down ever since. Just because there was an ad in the paper to buy 'em out don't mean he's gonna murder 'em if they don't sell to him."

I knew there was no point in telling them what Kramer said to me. I had no witnesses and Kramer would deny it, but I did have one ace to play. I said, "I heard something else. The story is that Kramer is bringing in his old crew from his Las Animas County spread and he'll let all of you go. The only reason he's held them back is that he wanted Pappy to think he was keeping his word."

That stopped them. I think they suspected this all the time, but they didn't want to believe it until they had to. They stared at me, but no one said a word except McGraw who muttered, "Where do we find jobs this time of year?"

I had been watching the bunkhouse door while we'd been talking, knowing that time was running out for me. Kramer and Hirsch came out of the bunkhouse. I stepped away from Larson and called, "Hirsch, I'm taking you in for the murder of Gramp Campbell."

They stopped, surprised, then Kramer said, "You ain't taking him nowhere, kid. If you think you can, make your play."

I started toward them, the certainty hammering at me that what Larson and McGraw did behind my back would determine whether I lived through the next five minutes. I said, "Kramer, I know damned well that you're responsible for Campbell's death. When I get a little more evidence, I'm coming after you. Right now Hirsch will do."

Hirsch had found a gun and was wearing it in his right-hand holster, but I had a hunch he wouldn't use it unless I forced him. The man was scared. It was written all over him. He'd been plenty brash yesterday, but at that time he hadn't been wanted for murder. He glanced at Kramer who had moved to my right so he stood a good ten feet from Hirsch. His right hand was close to his gun butt. If I didn't get any backing, I'd try for Kramer, then for Hirsch. If it came down to that, Hirsch would make his try, but I figured Kramer was the fast one. The problem was that even if I got lucky with Kramer, Hirsch would have all the time in the world to make his play.

I walked slowly toward them, my right hand almost touching the butt of my gun, but not quite. The instant I did, guns would blaze and there would be some dead men on the ground. When I was about twenty feet from them I said, "I want your gun, Hirsch."

Kramer's gaze had been pinned on me. Now Larson said, "Kramer, stay out of it. I'll drop you if you make a move toward your gun."

They were the most welcome words I'd ever heard in my life. Kramer's eyes swung to Larson, an expression of absolute courage on his face. "By God, Larson, what side are you on? Are you working for Anchor or not?"

"I'm not on any side," Larson said. "I say this ain't none of your put-in. I ain't gonna stand still while you gun down a lawman. He's all we've got in Turner County. Now about me working for Anchor, I don't know. You ain't said a word about it since you got here."

"You sure as hell ain't working for me now," Kramer bellowed. I won't stand for one of my men turning against me. Roll up your soogans and light a shuck off this spread."

I had moved up so that now I stood beside Hirsch. I lifted his gun from leather and jerked my head toward the corral. "Sandy, will you saddle this man's horse? Hirsch, you meander toward the corral."

"I didn't kill nobody," Hirsch cried out in a tone of despair. "Soon as you got out of sight I turned around and came here. I've been here ever since. I couldn't have killed nobody."

"What time was the old man killed?" Larson asked.

"I don't know exactly," I answered. "Bud Campbell rode to town to get me and the preacher and Doc. It was about dusk when he got there. He didn't leave home right away. He carried the body into the house and then rode over to my folks' place. He came to town after that. It must have been five, six o'clock when Campbell was killed."

"I was here," Hirsch cried. "They all saw me."

Kramer wasn't saying anything. I prodded Hirsch in the back with my gun. He started toward his horse that McGraw had saddled, stumbling and crying like a small boy. When we reached his horse, Larson said, "He's lying, Ed. He didn't ride in here until after dark. He had plenty of time to kill the old man."

"I didn't kill him," Hirsch whimpered. "I tell you I didn't kill nobody."

"Get on your horse," I said. "I'll listen to your story when we get to town."

I shoved the barrel of his gun under my waistband and stepped into the saddle. Hirsch held to the horn of his saddle, for a moment, swaying and trembling until he wasn't sure if he had the strength to lift himself into the saddle. He did finally. I glanced at Kramer who was still standing in front of the bunkhouse, his face as dark as any thundercloud I had ever seen.

"I'll see you in town, Ed," Larson said. "I guess I've got the answer to my question."

"Thanks, Lars," I said. "I'd be dead by now if it hadn't been for you."

"I think you would be," he said. "I guess I just couldn't let the law down."

"Let's get moving," I said to Hirsch.

When we rode away, Kramer still hadn't moved. I remembered he was to be in town at one. I'd hear from him then. I knew it as well as if I'd heard it in words. He was not a man to stand still after he'd been humiliated as he had been this morning. Whether he'd make a move by himself or wait for his crew to ride in was something for me to worry about.

Chapter XIX

Neither Hirsch nor I said a word all the way to town until we rode through the archway of the livery stable and dismounted. Hubey came running in from the back. When he saw whom I'd brought in, I thought his eyes would pop out of his head.

"So you fetched him back," he said.

"This time to jail," I said. "Gramp Campbell might be alive now if I'd locked him up yesterday when I had a chance."

"You figger he beefed the old man?" Hubey asked.

"Looks like it," I said. "Take care of the horses, Hubey. We're going to have a little talk before I lock him up."

"You bet," Hubey said.

"Come on," I said to Hirsch. "The jail isn't far from here. If you try to run, you'll be on the ground before you know it."

His ugly face seemed uglier than ever. He was sulking but he was still scared. Scared enough to talk, I thought. He walked along docilely enough. When we went into the jail, I motioned toward a chair.

"Sit down, Hirsch," I said. "It's more

comfortable out here than in a cell."

He sat down and glared at me, trying to keep a tough front, but as I moved around my desk and dropped into my swivel chair, his facade broke and he almost screamed at me. "My God, what have I got to do to prove I didn't kill the old man?"

"Right now you can talk," I said. "You've got some answers to questions that have been bothering me ever since I heard about Dan Kramer. You can start off by telling me what you were supposed to do for him."

"Nothing," he said sullenly. "Nothing that was a crime." He stared at the floor for a few seconds, then mumbled, "I knew there was a big ranch somewhere close to where you left me, so I started looking for it. I didn't find it till after dark. They put me up and gave me a couple of meals. If you hadn't got there when you did, I'd have been gone and I wouldn't be sitting here in your stinking jail."

From where I sat I could see that his boots were far from new and that he had small feet, so I could count him out as the killer. I had been reasonably certain he wasn't but whether he was or not, I'd hold him for the Las Animas County sheriff.

I rose. "Well, if you don't want to help

yourself, I'll lock you up. The judge is out of town, but he'll be back in a few days and you'll have a quick trial. Everybody liked Gramp Campbell, including the judge. I figure we'll get a gallows built and wind it up in a few days." I motioned toward the cells. "Come on."

"Wait a minute." The bravado had gone out of him. His face had turned pale, the fear that he had tried to control now overwhelming him. "I don't know much. All I can tell you is what I was supposed to do. Kramer hadn't paid me. That's why I came back. If it hadn't been for that, I'd have kept right on riding."

"I know you're wanted in Trinidad for fraud," I said. "I also know that you're an actor. I'll hold you until I hear from the Trinidad sheriff. But serving a term for fraud is a hell of a lot better than hanging for murder."

"Yeah." He swallowed, still staring at the floor as if unable to make up his mind as to how much he should tell. Finally he looked up at me. "How'd you find out all that?"

"It's on a reward dodger about you," I said. "I suppose you were trying to make us think you're Buck Sharkey and scare us to death."

His face lighted up and I thought he was

going to laugh. "Buck Sharkey is a myth. Suckers like you don't know that. Every paid killer in the West for years has claimed be Buck Sharkey. Fact is, there's a dozen Buck Sharkeys."

I wasn't really surprised. That thought had occurred to me as being a useful device for professional assassins to hide their identity. I said, "You were play-acting then, adding your little bit to the Buck Sharkey legend?"

He nodded. "That's right. I was wanted in Trinidad so I dropped out of sight. I had friends who were hiding me. I'd been in several plays, so I was pretty well known around town. But you've got to believe me when I say I don't know what Kramer's game is. All I know is that he quizzed around until he found the right people and got word to me that he had a job that would pay five hundred dollars. My friends passed the information along to me.

"I'd heard of him, but I'd never met the man. He got together with me late one night. He told me all he wanted me to do was to pretend to be a gunman and ride into Purgatory. I wasn't to do anything. Just show myself. Let people see me. Talk to 'em. Stay in town twenty-four hours and then ride out. He said he'd be at Anchor and for me to stop on my way out of the county and I'd get paid. He gave me money to buy a horse, these clothes and two guns. I didn't have anything but town duds."

He stopped and stared at me as if wondering whether I believed him. For some reason I did. It proved what I had been thinking, that Kramer in his devious way had used the man for a decoy. I leaned back in my chair thinking about it.

After a time I said, "You were to call yourself Buck Smith and let people draw their own conclusion about who you were. It was all the better if we thought you were Sharkey."

He nodded. "That's right, but I had no idea that murder was a part of Kramer's plan. I wouldn't have touched it if I'd had a hint of that."

"You still don't know what Kramer's scheme is?"

He shook his head. "Not a thing about it. I tried to quiz him, but he told me the less I knew, the better off I was, that all I had to do was to play the part and get out of town. I suppose I was stupid not to guess that I was being used for a hell of a lot more than Kramer said."

"It does seem you were pretty gullible," I said. "When anybody plays the part of a

gunman, he's running a chance that someone is going to let him prove how good he
is."

"I know that," he said, "but when you're
hungry enough you'll try anything for five
hundred dollars. Kramer said I wasn't to
ruffle anybody and to stay out of trouble. I
figured I'd be out of town before any
ruckus kicked up in my face. I sure as hell
didn't expect to run into an edgy kid
sheriff. In fact, Kramer said the sheriff was
an old man stove up with rheumatiz and he
wouldn't give me any trouble."

"It was that way a few days ago," I said.

Hirsch scowled at me for a moment,
then he said in an apologetic tone, "I was
pretty sore yesterday. I didn't want to lose
my guns and I didn't want Kramer to say I
hadn't earned my money. I guess I said
some things I shouldn't have."

"Where'd you get the gun you were
wearing this morning?" I asked.

"Kramer gave it to me," he answered.
"He said I might need it before I got out of
the county. I didn't want to take it, figuring
that a gun can get a man into a pile of
trouble and I was supposed to be finished
playing the gunman role, but Kramer insisted."

He stopped suddenly as if a new and terrifying thought had just struck him. "Say, do you suppose he thought you'd kill me if I was armed? I'd be out of the way and couldn't do any talking? Not that I know anything, but he's a careful man."

"Maybe," I said, thinking that Kramer might very well have had such a notion. "Did he ever mention Simon Ross to you?"

Hirsch shook his head. "Never heard the name."

"You know anything about Kramer's old crew?" I asked.

"I didn't hear anything about it," he answered, "but when I rode in yesterday I passed a bunch of men camped along the river. Six of 'em. Sure looked like hard cases to me."

"You sure this is all you can tell me?" I asked.

"That's it," he said.

I locked him in a cell and, opening the gun cabinet, laid the last gun I'd taken from him beside the other two I'd taken from him yesterday. I locked the cabinet, thinking that Hirsch wasn't a stupid man. He surely had known that he was playing a dangerous role, so he must have been hungry to have taken the job.

I sat down at my desk, thinking about

Kramer and trying to figure out what his next move would be. He probably wouldn't order another killing until he'd talked to the west side ranchers today at the bank. If they still would take his offer, then someone else would die, and I still felt that the odds were good it would be Pa.

The fear for Pa's safety had been in my mind for hours and I simply could not think of any way I could protect him. I could go out to where the killer had hidden along the river and wait for him to show up, but I had no way of knowing where he would hide the next time. I'd be wasting my effort and be out of town when I should be here.

I might just as well butt heads with Kramer now. I felt like a man waiting for the other shoe to drop. Or, more fitting would be the case of a man in a boat about to go over a falls. I had never been patient and today I found waiting unbearable.

If Kramer didn't come after me, maybe I could be obnoxious enough to force him to make a move. I would be at the bank at one o'clock. I'd talk to every rancher who showed up and urge him not to sell. I'd be loud enough for Kramer to hear me. That would do it, I thought.

Of course I still didn't know just how

Kramer would handle himself, and I didn't know how fast he was on the draw, but he struck me as being competent at anything he attempted. He had come close to drawing on me this morning and he would have if Larson hadn't backed me up.

I guessed from what had happened at Anchor that Kramer was reasonably sure he could take me. Caroline had been certain he would get rid of me one way or another. I decided right then I'd rather die with my killer in front of me than the way Gramp Campbell had.

Suddenly I thought of the plans I had made during the night when I couldn't sleep. See Simon Ross! I jumped up and left the jail, wondering how I could have forgotten. I wasn't sure Ross would tell me any more than Hirsch had, but I was going to enjoy making him tell me anything he could.

When I remembered how God-damned superior he had been when he'd gone into his office that morning, using me as a door mat to wipe his feet on, my sense of anticipation grew. He was a pompous man of great pride and dignity. Before I was done, I would strip him of both.

Chapter XX

I ran around the courthouse and along the boardwalk until I was opposite the bank, driven by a feeling that this was something I could do now, something I didn't have to wait for. I'd had a feeling of frustration too long, a sense of not being on top of what was happening.

I crossed the nearly deserted street and went into the bank. Alec Simpson, the teller, was sitting at his desk working on a ledger. He glanced up and frowned as I strode past the counter to the door that opened into Ross's private office.

"You can't go in until I announce you," Simpson shouted in an anxious tone as if knowing Ross would give him hell for letting me go in.

"You stay put," I said. "I'll announce myself."

I opened the office door and went through it. Ross was standing by a window looking across an empty lot toward the street, his hands jammed into his pockets. He whirled when he heard me. The instant he saw who had come in, an expression of distaste swept over his face. Or perhaps one of loathing. Whatever his exact feelings were, I didn't doubt that he had no use for me whatever.

"Get out of here, Logan," he snapped. "I'm a busy man. I have no time to listen to your problems."

"I'm not here to talk about my problems," I said. "It's your problem, and in case you didn't know it, you've got a big one."

I dragged a chair to the door and propped it under the knob. I didn't want Simpson or anyone else coming in until I was finished with Ross.

When he saw what I was doing, he screamed like a woman, "What are you doing?"

"We're going to have a quiet little talk," I said. "I don't aim to be interrupted. Now you sit down behind your desk and start answering some questions that I don't have the answers for."

He ran to his desk. He didn't walk. He actually ran, his short legs pumping hard. He grabbed the handle of a desk drawer, jerked it open and came up with a revolver. He pointed it at me, but I'd had a hunch what he'd try to do, so I was only a step behind him. I twisted the gun out of his hand and tossed it across the room.

"Now that's downright unfriendly, Ross," I said. "You forget that I'm a lawman and I'm supposed to use a gun, not you."

He leaned back in his chair and glared at me, so furious that for a few seconds he couldn't get a word out, then he started to curse me. I slapped him across the side of his face, a hard blow that rocked his head and left that side of his face red.

"I said we'd talk," I told him. "That doesn't mean for me to stand still and listen to you cuss me."

He sat as if paralyzed, an expression of sheer amazement on his face. I guessed he had never been struck in anger before in his life, at least not since he'd been a kid. Apparently now he simply couldn't believe that I'd hit him.

He whispered, "You'll pay for what you just did, Logan. By God, I'll have you drummed out of town. I'll have the law on you and I'll —"

"No you won't," I said. "Funny how you keep forgetting that I am the law."

I stood at the end of the desk, waiting to see if he was ready to quiet down and answer my questions. He placed both hands on the desk in front of him and formed them into fists and stared at them, not looking at me or even recognizing my presence. A vein throbbed in his forehead, a muscle twitched in his cheek, and for a moment I wondered if he was going to have a stroke.

I moved to the front of the desk and pulled a chair up to it and sat down. I asked, "Now are you going to answer my questions?"

He still didn't say anything or look at me. The red had faded from the cheek where I had slapped him. His face was as gray as death, but the veins in his forehead had stopped throbbing and I thought the twitch in his cheek was not bad. He'd be all right, I thought. I don't believe I'd have had much sympathy for him if he'd had a stroke. I couldn't forget what he'd done to Pa and some of our neighbors. I knew of at least one rancher who had shot himself because the bank had foreclosed on his spread.

"Ross," I said, "you've manipulated the people of this county as long as I can remember, usually to their loss and your gain. You're mean and little and selfish, and above all things you love money. You've used the bank and the credit you dole out as a weapon to control what goes on.

"The only men you ever listened to were Judge Willoughby and Pappy Jordan. Now Pappy's gone and the man who has taken his place is just like you except that he is a very tough hombre. You plan to use him to give you strength and he plans to use you to help him make a fortune. I want to know what your plan is."

He heard me, all right, but he still wouldn't look at me and he still wouldn't talk. Losing my patience, I shouted, "Damn it, Ross, you'd better talk to me here or I'll throw you in jail as an accessory to murder."

The words changed everything. His head snapped back and he stared at me. "You wouldn't dare, Logan," he whispered. "You've come in here and locked everyone else out and you've insulted me and you've struck me, but putting me in jail is more than even a man with a depraved mind like yours would do."

"Try me," I said. "Murder is a crime that even you can't get away with."

The tip of his tongue darted out of his mouth and moistened his dry lips. "I haven't had anything to do with murder. What are you talking about?"

"I'm talking about the murder of Gramp Campbell," I said.

"My God, Logan," he said in a strained voice. "I had nothing to do with that. I was home yesterday from the time I left the bank until I came back this morning. Elvira will testify to that."

"I never accused you of committing the murder," I said. "I am accusing you of plotting it with Dan Kramer. He has invited the west side ranchers to come to your bank at one o'clock today to sell their outfits. If they don't sell, there will be another killing to make his offer stick. Now I've been told that you have a working agreement with him. That sure as hell makes you a partner in whatever crime he has committed."

He sat frozen, his gaze on my face. "I don't know anything about the crimes you say he has committed. I did not plot any crimes with him." He swallowed, then asked, "Do you have proof that Kramer killed the old man?"

"He didn't pull the trigger any more than you did," I said. "Someone he hired did. I have a man in jail now that I thought was the killer, but I don't think so now. I'll find the man who did it, then I'll get the proof that Kramer was the one who paid for the murder, but right now it might help if you told me what you know."

He licked his lips again, then he said, "You can't convince me that Kramer had anything to do with Campbell's murder."

"I'm not trying to convince you," I said, impatience gnawing at me again. "I'm convinced, and I'll convince a jury. You won't believe this, either, but Kramer told me that he'd kill some of the west side ranchers to scare the others into selling. The only thing I don't know is what his scheme is. He seems to be in one hell of a hurry. Now tell me why he is willing to run the risk of hiring one or more killings in order to get the whole valley?"

Ross took a long breath, then he said slowly, "I don't know, Logan. So help me, I don't know. He walked in here several weeks ago when he'd come to the county to look Anchor over. He intended to buy the outfit, but he hadn't agreed with Jordan on a price. He said he would and he wanted to work with me in controlling county affairs for his protection and my profit.

"He said he intended to buy the west side ranchers out because he felt that the entire valley could be operated as one spread more efficiently than it was now. He admitted that some of his tactics would not be exactly legal, but he never hinted that murder was one of those tactics."

I didn't say anything for a time. I sat motionless, thinking about what Ross had said. I believed it. Probably Kramer wouldn't tell him exactly what he planned. It would be enough to dangle more profit under the banker's nose. He was money hungry enough to accept almost anything if it did indeed promise more profit and eventually more power. Ross was glad to get rid of Pappy Jordan, and he probably thought he could handle Judge Willoughby with Jordan gone. In any case, as old as the Judge was, he wouldn't likely be a problem for Ross much longer.

"All right," I said. "Maybe you're telling the truth. One more question. Why have you insisted on getting me out of the sheriff's office before you found out whether I could handle the job or not? You even backed Moran. You knew he would be as inefficient as old man York was."

"I know," Ross said. "When Kramer came in the first time, he asked about the sheriff. I said he was old and bunged up with rheumatiz and wouldn't be an obstacle to whatever Kramer planned. When York was killed, I wanted Moran because he'd be easy to handle. I knew you were a smart aleck kid who'd throw his weight around and wouldn't listen to reason. I was trying to make it easier for Kramer. I wanted to show him I could be of help to him, but I tell you, I never dreamed that murder was part of his plan."

I almost laughed when he said I wouldn't listen to reason. If bucking Kramer's dirty work and Ross's greed was refusing to listen to reason, then I was guilty. I said, "It doesn't strike me that Kramer is a reasonable man. Or you, either."

He shifted his weight in his chair, glanced at me, then looked away. "You're not going to lock me up, are you?"

I would have said under other circumstances that he was a pathetic little man who was scared out of his pants and was reduced to begging from someone he had called "a smart aleck kid." Somehow the word pathetic had never seemed to fit Simon Ross. I remembered I had thought about stripping him of his pride and his dignity. I had done exactly that, but now that I had done it, I didn't feel much satisfaction in my accomplishment. He was a miserable little man, scared and helpless, a man stripped of the veneer of strength and power that he had kept wrapped around him.

"I'll think about that," I said and rose. "Right now Kramer is the man I've got to stop."

I walked to the door, moved the chair and opened the door. I left the office and crossed the lobby in long strides. Alec Simpson watched me with concern, but I didn't stop or say anything to him. As I went out through the door, I had a strange feeling about my visit with Ross, an unpleasant feeling, a feeling as repulsive as if I had been turning rocks over and finding slimy and ugly things underneath. I hoped that in the future I would never as long as I lived have anything to do with Simon Ross again. What made it worse was the fact that I had not learned much that I hadn't known before.

I stepped across the boardwalk and into the fall sunshine that was not as warm as it had been through the last pleasant Indian summer days. In another hour or two the sunshine would be gone. Storm clouds that had been hanging down over the mountains were moving eastward and would soon cover the sky. We'd have the snow I had been expecting before morning.

"Ed."

It was Bud Campbell's voice. He had just come out of the hotel. Now, as he ran toward me, I sensed from the drawn expression on his face that the worst had happened. I guess I knew before he said another word that it had happened just as I had been expecting it to happen.

"I've been looking all over for you," Bud called.

I stood frozen in the middle of the street. Bud came on to me, breathing hard. "Your Pa was shot about an hour ago. He ain't dead. He was shot in the head and he's unconscious. Doc's on his way out there now. I told Hubey to saddle your horse."

For a moment I stood there, my mind refusing to function. I had known this would happen. I had not been able to prevent it. I had warned Pa. Still it had happened. It would be like Kramer to pick the father of a troublesome sheriff for his second killing.

Then I came out of it. Hubey led Alexander out of the livery stable. I ran to him, swung into the saddle and left town on the run.

Chapter XXI

I rode Alexander harder than he had ever been ridden before in his life. I knew because I had raised him from a colt. He was lathered and heaving when I reined up in front of our house. I hit the ground running, raced up the path to the front door and then stopped, knowing that I couldn't charge into the house. I'd upset Ma more than she was upset now.

I crossed the living room slowly and stepped in the doorway, hardly breathing because I didn't know what to expect. Doc was finishing putting a bandage on Pa's head. Ma was standing near the foot of the bed watching the doctor. Caleb Watts was standing back of the doctor. When he glanced toward the door and saw me he walked quickly to me. My gaze was on Pa. I was surprised and relieved to see that he was conscious.

Caleb laid a hand on my shoulder. "He's going to be all right unless some complications develop and Doc doesn't expect any." He nodded toward the bed. "He's been asking for you. You'd better speak to him, then I'll tell you what I know about how it happened."

I walked toward the bed. When Ma saw me, she put an arm around him. She had been crying, but she wasn't now. She said, "I'm so glad you're here, Ed. He's been wanting to see you."

Doc stepped back as he said, "Ed's here, Abner. Don't move your head. Just move your eyes. It's very important that you don't move your head."

Pa's eyes turned enough so I knew he was looking at me. He whispered, "I'm glad you're here, Ed. They keep telling me I'll be all right, but I ain't so sure about it."

He lifted a hand and I took it, surprised because I didn't remember him ever showing much physical affection. I was close to crying, but I managed to say, "I'm sorry, Pa. I'm so damned sorry. I should have stopped it."

"It ain't your fault, son," he said. "You can't keep an eye on all outdoors. That's why I wanted to see you. I knew you'd blame yourself. You warned me it might happen."

"I'll get the man who did it, Pa," I said. "That's a promise."

"That's something else I wanted to tell you," Pa said. "Getting the man who done it ain't so important. Staying alive is. If I go, you've got to take care of your Ma."

"I will," I said. "That's another promise."

"Enough talk," Doc Wardell broke in. "You sit her beside the bed, Mrs. Logan. The rest of you clear out. I want him to stay quiet and not even talk."

Caleb had moved into the living room. Doc walked out of the bedroom, and I followed. When we were far enough from the bed so Pa couldn't hear us talk, Doc said, "I'm glad you got here, Ed. For some reason Abner thought he had to see you. He kept mumbling something about being too hard on you. He didn't want you to blame yourself for what happened. Said he wouldn't have got shot if he'd stayed inside like you told him to do."

"He couldn't have done it any more than Gramp Campbell could," I said. "I knew that when I told him to stay inside. The only way I could have stopped him was to have stayed home and done the work, and I couldn't do that after I put on this God-damned star."

"It's been hell," Wardell admitted, "but I honestly think, Ed, that you are the only man in the county who can do this job. You will, too. It may get worse before it gets any better, but you'll get your man."

I still felt like crying, but Doc's words helped. I swallowed and glanced at Caleb who nodded in agreement. "It's hard to believe these things are happening to Turner County," he said. "It may sound crazy, but the truth is we're in a war. When a man finds himself in that situation, he has to do things he wouldn't have done otherwise, even to neglecting what he might think of as his duties in normal conditions."

At the moment I wasn't thinking straight. The only thing I knew was that I was going to jail Dan Kramer and I'd beat him until he signed a confession. Afterwards when I had time to think about the events of a day that was not like any other day of my life, I knew what Caleb meant. Of course he was right. Normally I would have stayed home and done my best to comfort Ma, but not today. It was in no way a normal day.

"I've got to get back to town," Doc said. "Mrs. Gibbs may be having her baby right now. There's nothing more I can do for Abner. As far as I can tell, he'll be all right if he takes it easy. He'll have to stay in bed. I know he'll be faunching around about the work, but it'll have to go for a few days."

"If I can't come back to stay tonight," I said, "I'll get a neighbor kid to come in and do the chores."

Wardell nodded. "Good. Several things may or could happen to him. Headaches. Dizziness. Fuzzy thinking. A head wound is always tricky, but if he stays quiet maybe he'll avoid all of those aftereffects."

He left the house, untied his mare and rode back to town. I walked out of the house and stood in the doorway watching him, but my thoughts were on Pa, a man who had demanded so much of himself and of me and anyone else who worked for him, a man who could thumb his nose at Simon Ross when the banker turned down his request for a loan and go right on making a living.

Now all of this was changed. He was helpless, absolutely dependent on others as much as a baby would be. That was bound to gall him. Suddenly the tears came and I could not hold back the sobs that shook my entire body. It was when I thought about him wanting to see me to tell me not to blame myself that I broke down.

I thought about the afternoon of my birthday when Judge Willoughby had come out to ask me to serve as sheriff and Pa had been hell-bent on finishing the day's work and I thought I hated him. Now I knew I hadn't: it was his way and he could not change it or himself if he wanted. I knew I didn't hate him at all. I loved him very much. I realized he had always done the best he could under the circumstances and the knowledge he had at any particular time.

I yanked my bandanna out and wiped my eyes and blew my nose. I couldn't remember crying since I'd been a child and had been whipped or when I was frustrated over something I wanted and couldn't have. When I had myself under control, I looked at Caleb who had followed me and stood a few feet from me.

"Tell me what happened," I said.

He nodded. "First I want to say I'm glad you could cry. It relaxed you. It was right and proper that you should. Some men never can cry and they become emotional cripples because of it."

I didn't fully grasp what he was saying then any more than I had before. Caleb was that way sometimes but I never argued or questioned him. Usually when I thought about it later, I was able to make some sense out of what he'd said. He was a very unusual man and I was glad he was my friend. I guess he simply lived above and beyond the plane that most of us live on.

"Now about what happened," Caleb went on. "Your ma wasn't able to talk very much, but I gathered that she was in the kitchen when she heard the shot. She doesn't know where it came from, but she thought it was from the side of the hill above the house. She ran out and dragged your pa around the corner so he wouldn't be in sight of the killer, then she saddled a horse and rode to the Campbell place.

"Bud came back with her and he carried your pa inside, then he lit out for town. She's been right beside your pa ever since. She was badly frightened because your pa bled so much. Now it's in the hands of the Lord, but your ma will give him all the attention any human can give, so we have every reason to think he'll be all right."

I nodded, knowing that she would. I went back into the house and for a moment stood in the doorway staring at Pa's motionless form on the bed. Ma rose and came to me. She said, "I guess he's gone to sleep. Doc gave him something to keep him quiet."

"He'll be all right," I said, looking at the bloody bandage around his head, at his pale, almost lifeless face, and wondering if I was lying to her. We were all trying to assure each other, I thought, and none of us knew a damned thing about what was going to happen.

"We have to trust in God," she said.

I nodded, wondering how big a part God played in a situation like this. I said, "I've got to get back to town. I'm still the sheriff."

She turned to me and put her arms around me and buried her face in the front of my shirt. "I know, Ed," she said, "and I wish you weren't. It's like Pa said. The important thing is for you to stay alive. I couldn't bear it if Pa died and you were killed. If Pa didn't make it, you'd be all I had."

I didn't tell her that I was going to jail Dan Kramer if I lived long enough to do it. I had a strong hunch I wouldn't. He would never surrender without a fight and I didn't have the slightest hope I could outdraw the man. Maybe I could get the drop on him, but that wasn't likely. He was a hard man, but he was also a careful one, and he had no intention of dying.

"I know, Ma," I said. "I'll be careful."

She hugged and kissed me. I turned and walked out of the house. Caleb was still standing on the porch. He said, "I'll stay a little longer, but I can't stay long. There are some things in town I have to do."

We walked along the path to the hitching post in front of the house. I stepped into the saddle and said, "We appreciate your coming out."

"I always feel my weakness at a time like this," he said. "There's just not much a man can do except to pray and stand by to show I care." He hesitated, then he added, "There's one thing I want to mention before you leave. Sharon saw me early this morning. She asked me to marry you two tomorrow. I can, of course, if you want it done then."

"We'd better wait," I said. "Pa would want to be there. I'll talk to her today."

He nodded gravely, then he said, "Ed, I know you're determined to bring the assassin to justice and that's the way it should be, but you need help. Some of us would be glad to serve as unofficial deputies. There's no law that says the sheriff has to do everything by himself."

"No, there isn't," I agreed, "but I'm not very good at asking for help. Besides, when a man pins on a star, he knows the risk he's taking. You've got a wife and . . ."

"Oh hell," he said angrily, then grinned shamefacedly. "That didn't sound good coming from a preacher, did it? What I want to say is that Sharon needs you as much as my wife needs me. I felt that very much when she talked to me. Besides, you've got your ma to think about and your pa's —"

"I'll call on you if I need you," I broke in, and reining Alexander around, I rode away.

I was a little irritated with Caleb worrying so much about my welfare. I could understand Pa's and Ma's concern, but Caleb's interest was too much. He acted as if he thought I couldn't handle it and that put a burr under my saddle. I was aware I was being foolish because the odds were he was dead right. Still, I felt that I couldn't ask a married man to risk his life helping me do my job.

I reached the Campbell place before I realized it. I heard Bud yell at me and I pulled up. He came running toward me, so I waited. When he reached me, he said, "There's something I didn't think to tell you in town. Didn't have time anyway, but I thought you'd better know though maybe it ain't nothing. I heard the shot that got your pa. I was riding south of here. Thought I might find out something about the bastard that shot Gramp. Or maybe I just had to get away from here for a while."

He choked up for a few seconds. I waited, thinking that getting away for a while was the real reason he was out riding. I was remembering that when I'd asked him to serve as my deputy, he had turned me down flat. My best friend, the one man I had thought I could depend on.

I realized, then, that this was the real reason I didn't want to ask Caleb or anyone else for help. If I couldn't get it from Bud, I couldn't expect to get it from anyone else. The truth was I was afraid I'd be turned down again. Staring at Bud's pale, upturned face, I knew our days of friendship were over.

"Anyhow, I barely heard the shot," Bud went on after he had his feelings under control. "I lit out for home, figuring that someone else had been killed. I knew the shot had come from the hill above us, but I didn't see nobody and I didn't see no gunsmoke. I kept watching the hill and pretty soon I saw a man riding along the fringe of timber. I don't have no proof he was the one who fired the shot, but I figured there wasn't no reason for a stranger to be riding up there."

"A stranger?" I asked. "You sure?"

"Hell yes," Bud said. "Nobody dresses like that around here just to go riding. He had a suit on and he was wearing a derby hat, but he rode like he'd been on a horse all his life."

Charlie Lambert! It had to be him. Sure, I'd thought of him being the killer, but not for long. The only reason I'd even given him a minute's thought was the fact that he was a stranger and had arrived in Purgatory about the time Kramer and Hirsch had. I'd been so convinced that he was what he'd said he was, a treasure hunter, that I'd overlooked him. He just didn't fit the mental picture I held of a gunman.

"Thanks, Bud," I said. "I know the man."

I rode on, irritation at my stupidity growing in me, but another thought crowded that one out of my mind. Lambert would either leave the county after shooting Pa or he'd back Kramer up when Kramer came after my scalp. Knowing how careful Kramer was, I decided he'd keep Lambert here as insurance, and that made any chance I had of taking Kramer slightly less than zero.

I glanced up at the sun and realized it must be after noon and the west side ranchers were supposed to meet at the bank to sell out to Kramer at one o'clock. I put Alexander into a gallop, telling myself I had to be at the bank in time to stop the sales that Kramer wanted to force. He'd be there, I thought glumly, and that would be the hour of reckoning.

Chapter XXII

When I reached town I saw a knot of men, six or eight, gathered in front of the bank. When I reined into the livery stable, Hubey saw me and ran toward me, yelling, "That Kramer fellow, you know, the one who bought Anchor, well, he's in town and he's looking for you."

I dismounted, thinking that was a crazy kind of a twist; Kramer looking for me at the same time I was looking for him. I asked, "Where is he?"

"He went into the hotel for dinner while ago," Hubey said. "I ain't seen him since. Another man's with him, that Lambert hombre who's been renting a horse every day since he got here."

I turned toward the archway, my stomach dropping about six inches into my gut. I didn't have the slightest idea how I could handle this. I had been hoping that Lambert would stay out of town and I'd have a chance at Kramer alone, but I guess I had known all the time that it would be that way.

Kramer was not a gambler. I had some

questions about Kramer's makeup, but none about this particular trait. He was simply an extraordinarily careful man. I could think of a lot of adjectives that fitted him, but above everything else was that one dominating characteristic. He was not one to take chances. As I crossed the dust strip to the bank, one terrifying thought pounded through my mind. I could not arrest Kramer until I got past Lambert.

Of the men who were gathered in front of the bank, I knew some casually, some well. I had worked with most of them at one time or another, during round-up or haying or threshing, or had simply exchanged work when we had needed an extra man for some heavy job.

More than that, and this was probably a better way of knowing what was really in a man, I had played baseball with a number of them, mostly on the town team. I had gone to church with them, too, and I'd seen practically all of them once a month at the dances over at Mark Vance's store. They were good, decent men, hardworking, typical small ranchers who ran a few head of cattle and did more farming than ranching.

As I approached them, they nodded at me and called greetings. I responded, all the time aware that until a few days ago we had been more or less equal. But now our relationship had changed, because of the star I wore. They seemed a little stand-offish. Another thought occurred to me. I could use a few heroes who would back me when I arrested Kramer and make sure I had a fair chance to take him, but I knew there wasn't a hero in the lot.

They had fanned out into a semicircle by the time I reached them. One said, "I heard about your pa. I'm sorry." Another asked, "How is he?"

"Doc said he'd make it if there aren't any complications," I answered.

I paused, my gaze moving from one end of the semicircle to the other. I sensed a feeling of uneasiness among them as if they were waiting for some calamity to happen. I asked, "You're all here to see Dan Kramer about selling your ranches?"

One of them nodded. The rest shifted their weight on their feet as if uneasy about their surrender. In reality, they had surrendered or they wouldn't be here. They were getting out. One killing and one near killing had done the job, but I still had to try to change their minds.

"Don't sell to him," I said. "Fight him. He's responsible for Gramp Campbell's killing and Pa's shooting. He's hired a man named Charlie Lambert to pull the trigger, figuring some killings would scare all of you into selling."

"Looked like it's done the job," one of them said bitterly. "We can't fight a dry gulcher who hides in the brush and don't give us a chance to fight back."

"You're the sheriff," one of them said accusingly. "Why ain't you arresting these men if you know so much about what they've done?"

"I aim to," I said. "If it was just Kramer, I'd go after him, but Lambert's in town, too, and he's a professional gunman. I figure there's a good chance he's really Buck Sharkey. I can't take both of them."

They shifted around again, their eyes on the ground. They knew what they ought to do, but they weren't brave enough to do it. I said, anger putting a bite to my words, "Go on home. You've got a lifetime invested in your spreads. All of you like it here or you wouldn't have stayed. Kramer won't give you what your property's worth. You can't put a dollar value on your land anyhow. You've got too much of your sweat and blood invested in your homes to turn tail and run."

I'd made them sore. That was easy to see

from the way they looked at me. I'd made them face the truth and they didn't like what they saw. One of them, a young man named Dave Farris who wasn't much older than I was said harshly, "Damn it, Ed, you are the law. We've got a right to look to you for protection. If you didn't figure on giving it to us, you shouldn't have pinned on that star."

"You're dead right, Dave," I said, "but any or all of you have an obligation to serve as my deputy if and when I need one. I need one right now. Will you take the job?"

Farris backed off, his face turning pale. "I've got a wife and baby. I can't risk it. My wife wants to sell. She's been scared to death ever since we saw Kramer's ad in the newspaper and heard that old man Campbell was killed. The last thing she said when I left this morning was to take whatever he offered and not argue, that we'd leave the valley."

"But if you keep your spread," I said, "your wife would be proud of you and happy to stay, wouldn't she? She'd never leave if she had a choice, would she?"

He didn't answer. He backed up another step, unable to meet my gaze. I had known it would go this way, but still I was hurt and angry that it had actually happened and none of them would help.

"You're a bunch of yellow-bellied crawling things," I yelled in a frenzy of anger. "You've got more at stake in this than I have. I aim to protect you and I'll enforce the law, but it's the duty of every citizen to support the law in a showdown. This is a showdown. My life is on the line. Everything you've spent a lifetime working for is threatened. All I want from any of you is to go into the hotel with me and see that Lambert stays off my back while I arrest Kramer."

They were filled with shame. That was plain to read in their anguished faces, their stooped shoulders. They began edging away from me, staring at the dust of the street or looking past me at nothing.

Then Charlie Lambert's loud and bullying voice hammered against my ears, "Logan, I'm going to kill you."

I whipped around as the men in front of me stumbled over each other getting off the street and diving into the bank to get out of the way of stray bullets. I saw Lambert standing in front of Clancy's Bar smiling as if anticipating something he was going to enjoy.

Lambert was wearing his derby hat and

store suit the same as when I had talked to him in the hotel the day he had arrived in Purgatory, but he wasn't the same man. He had been very amiable and pleasant that day, but now he had a faintly sneering expression on his face, as if he knew he was my superior when it came to gunfighting. He might have been slapping at an irritating fly. I was a kid upstart he was going to put in his place, that place being a six-foot-deep hole in the ground. This, I thought, was the real Charlie Lambert.

As I stepped into the middle of the street, I saw that the tail of his coat was swept back so it wouldn't be in the way of his draw. My heart was pounding; I was just plain scared, and I began to tremble as a terrible feeling took hold of me that I could not control my muscles when the time came to draw my gun.

Lambert was in no hurry. He stepped off the walk into the dust of the street and then stopped, all the time keeping his eyes riveted on me. Then, suddenly, and I never knew why or how it happened, the fear left me and I stopped trembling. This was shaping up better than I had expected. At least I was facing Lambert and not having to fight two men at the same time as I had been afraid I would.

Lambert took another step, calling, "You turned out to be a damned nuisance, kid. I should have taken care of you the first day I was in town."

I suppose it was the way of a professional gunman to prolong the act before he killed a man, to stretch time out until his opponent's nerve breaks and hurries his draw and thereby wastes that precious fraction of a second that might mean life instead of death. I wasn't going to be hurried. I started walking slowly toward him, my right hand brushing the butt of my gun. The one thing I was resolved not to do was to be panicked into drawing before we were close enough to be in what was an effective range for me.

At a time like this, concentrating on what I had to do and keeping my gaze on his right shoulder, it was strange that I should be aware of sounds and smells that were entirely irrelevant: the smell of burning leaves, the sound of a rooster crowing, of a barking dog. Then I saw his right shoulder start to dip and I went for my gun.

I knew immediately he had outdrawn me as I swept my gun from leather and I saw his gun barrel come up and leveled. It was all happening very fast, but before he pulled the trigger, the blast of a double-barreled shotgun smashed into the taut silence. Lambert's gun hand froze as his gaze swung toward the hotel lobby door.

I fired, using that tiny interval of time before he realized his mistake and pulled the trigger. He got off his shot a split-second after I fired, but my slug hit him and his bullet only tugged at my shirt. Then I saw he was down, his gun dropping from his slack fingers, his derby hat falling off his head and rolling away.

I paced toward him as the dust rose up around him, kept him covered, not knowing how hard he had been hit. I did not risk a glance at the hotel doorway to see who had fired the shotgun and why.

Lambert wasn't quite dead when I reached him, but death was only seconds away. Blood bubbled in his lips and dripped down his chin. That strange taunting smile he'd had on his lips when he'd first called to me was still there. I wondered if he had known all the time that this would someday happen to him, that it was always the eventual fate of a gunfighter.

"I got beaten by a kid who's a hell of lot slower than I am," he breathed, "but you've got the guts it takes."

"Are you Buck Sharkey?" I asked.

"Sure," he whispered, so low I barely heard him. "The great Buck Sharkey. Why not?"

He died then, the smile still fixed on his lips. I still didn't know if he was lying, or if the legendary Buck Sharkey had actually died by my hand in the dust of Purgatory's Main Street.

Chapter XXIII

I did not turn from Lambert to the hotel until I was certain that he was dead. I was not sure where the shotgun blast had come from, but I thought it had been from the hotel doorway. The instant I turned to look, I saw I was right. Dan Kramer lay, belly down on the walk in front of the doorway, the top of his head literally blown off.

I recoiled in horror. Blood and brains were splattered all over the boards of the walk. For a short time I thought I was going to throw up. Having just killed one man and then seeing this gruesome sight was too much. I walked into the hotel, turning my head so I wouldn't see the body but I knew very well that I'd be seeing it in my mind for long time.

When I entered the lobby, Caroline Dallas was sitting in a chair just inside the door, her back to the wall. Her face was pasty white. I wouldn't have been surprised if she had started to vomit. Her shotgun lay across her lap. She was staring at the floor, but when I started toward her, she looked up.

"I told you I'd kill him when the right time came," she said defiantly. "This was the right time." She lowered her gaze to the floor again and asked, "You going to arrest me?"

"He'd better not."

I wheeled. Beulah Heston was standing in the dining room doorway, her hands on her ample hips, a pugnacious expression on her round face. She moved toward us, jerking her head toward the corpse on the walk.

"You wouldn't be alive this minute, Ed Logan, if she hadn't blasted Kramer's head off," Beulah said. "You didn't see what happened, did you?"

"No," I said. "I was busy."

"I know," she said. "You done a good job with Lambert. I didn't have no idea he was a gunslick, just seeing him around the hotel and serving his meals. He seemed like a real gentleman, but he must have been a paid killer or he wouldn't have jumped you the way he done."

"He was Kramer's man," I said, "but I still don't see . . ."

"No, you were busy like you said, so I'll tell you how it was." Beulah moved across the lobby and dropped a hand to Caroline's shoulder. "This girl bought into

266

your fight and saved your life. That Kramer gent was putting his chips down on a sure thing. He stood there in the doorway with his gun in his hand watching you. I don't know whether he aimed to cut you down just before you fired or he was gonna wait to see if Lambert done the job, but it looked to me like he was ready to pull the trigger when she blasted him. Either way, you'd have been dead because you didn't know anything about him standing there waiting to plug you."

I sat down beside Caroline, sweat breaking out all over me. She was right. I'd have been lying in the street not far from Lambert's body if Caroline hadn't let go with the shotgun. This bore out what I'd been telling myself all the time. Kramer believed in a sure thing. He couldn't even stay out of a fight in which I was matched against a professional gunman.

I guess I was, as Lambert had said, more of a nuisance than Kramer had expected me to be. Maybe he'd thought he had bluffed me out the first day he was in town when he'd faced me in the jail. In any case, he did not intend to lose the deals he wanted to make with the west side ranchers. When he saw me talking to them, he must have made up his mind that he was not going to let me ruin his carefully made plans.

"I guess I owe you a whole lot of thanks, Caroline," I said.

"Don't thank me," she said somberly. "I didn't do it for you. He'd earned it a long time ago."

"Don't make no never mind who she done it for," Beulah said. "The fact is she saved your life, Ed, so you can't arrest her."

"I can arrest her, all right," I said, "but I can't put her in jail. I've got Hirsch there now and the jail doesn't have any place for women. I'll have to hold her till Judge Willoughby gets back though." I looked at Caroline, wondering what I was going to do with her, then I said, "If you give me your word you'll stay in town I'll leave you in Beulah's custody."

Beulah scowled and said, "I ain't no jailer." I guess she changed her mind in a hurry, because she added, "All right, Sheriff, she can stay right here in the hotel the way she has been. I reckon she won't run off."

"No, I don't think she will," I said as I rose. "She's too smart to make a fugitive out of herself."

I started toward the door, but before I reached it Caroline said, "One more thing,

Sheriff. Kramer's old crew will be riding in before long. They're tough and mean, and they're loyal to him. They'll tear this town apart when they find out what happened. I've got my hide to think about. When they hear who shot him, they'll hang me."

"Then we'll have to stop them," I said.

As I walked out of the lobby, I didn't have the slightest idea how I was going to stop six hard cases who wanted to hang Caroline Dallas. I circled Kramer's body, again not looking at him any more than I had to. A circle of men surrounded Lambert's body. As I approached, Doc Wardell was telling some of them to carry the bodies to his office and he'd fix them for burying, adding that he didn't think the coffin should be opened at Kramer' funeral. Nobody would want to look at him.

When they realized that I had joined them, they fell silent, looking at me and then looking away. I started to say something about Kramer's crew, but before I could get a word out, Mark Vance said, "You sure made believers out of us, Ed. Nobody is going to call you a kid sheriff after this."

"No, they sure won't," Wardell said. "I've seen some fancy shooting in my day, but Ed's was as good as anybody's."

"I've always been able to hit what I shoot at," I said, "if I've got plenty of time, but if the shot that killed Kramer hadn't slowed Lambert up, I'd be cold meat right now."

I'm not sure they believed that, but they didn't argue. I went on, "I've got to ride out to Anchor and tell Mrs. Kramer what happened. I'll be gone for an hour or so. We're not out of trouble yet; Kramer's old crew is headed our way and when they hear what happened, they'll raise hell."

"How many are there?" Dave Farris asked. "Six, I think," I said, surprised that Farris would ask.

I was even more surprised when Farris said, "What you said to us while ago has been eating hell out of me, but you were right when you called us yellow-bellied crawling things or something like that. I want to give you a hand when they show up."

"Thanks, Dave," I said. "I'll need help if they start anything." I walked away then, thinking that Farris was talking through his hat, that he hadn't had any courage before when I asked for help and I didn't believe he'd found any since. He'd be gone by the time I got back from Anchor.

As I saddled Alexander, Hubey leaned his pitchfork against the wall of the stall and came down the runway toward me. He said, "You were great, Sheriff. I was sure scared when I saw Lambert coming at you. I guess you're the best sheriff Turner County ever had."

I swung into the saddle and looked down at the boy, his admiring eyes on me. I knew it had been a sort of hero worship from the first, but now it was more than that. If there was any help to be found in Purgatory when Kramer's crew rode into town, it would come from Hubey.

"I dunno about that," I said. "I don't think I'm that good." I hesitated, not wanting to get Hubey involved in what was going to happen in a few hours, but at the same time knowing that I had to do whatever I could to save Purgatory and I had a hunch Hubey would die fighting before the businessmen would.

Finally I asked, "Have you got any kind of gun here in the stable?"

"Yeah, I've got dad's old greener," he said. "I never have used it since I started working, but I kept it here in case I ever did need it. Why?"

"Kramer's old crew will be in town later today," I said. "Or I think they will be. When they hear about him being killed, they may go loco and burn the town down. We're going to have to show them that they can't do it. That's going to take more than my gun."

"That'll make me a sort of deputy, wouldn't it, Sheriff?" he said, his eyes shining.

"Yeah, I guess it would," I said.

"I'll load the shotgun and leave it right beside the door," he said.

"Good," I nodded. "But don't start anything by yourself. I figure I've got more than an hour before they show up. I'll be back before then."

"Oh, I wouldn't be loco enough to start a fight," he said, "but I'll sure be here if they start it."

I rode out through the archway and headed toward Anchor. I wasn't looking forward to telling Mrs. Kramer about her husband's death, but then, it was hard to tell how she'd take it. Maybe she'd be glad to hear he was dead.

As I rode, I thought about how my feelings were very much different than they had been after I'd shot Max Moran. I had not wanted to kill him, and it had been hard on me even though he had forced the fight. With Lambert I had no such regrets. When I considered Gramp Campbell's murder and Pa's shooting, I thought of him as nothing more than a mad dog.

Dan Kramer was no better. Then Caroline Dallas came into my mind. I wondered whether she had shot Kramer simply because he had been about to gun me down, or had I given her an excuse to do what she had come here to do without having to answer for murder? I would never know the answer, but there was a good deal about Caroline Dallas I would never know. She'd told me enough times that she was going to kill him. I was thankful she did the job at the exact moment she did.

Chapter XXIV

When I reached Anchor, I saw that Lars Larson and the crew were saddling up. I had a hunch that Kramer had fired the whole bunch before he'd left this morning, and I was afraid I'd miss them. Mrs. Kramer was sitting in her rocking chair on the front porch. She was the one I'd come see, but I decided I'd better talk to Larson before I saw her. I didn't want the crew riding off until I'd had a chance to talk to Mrs. Kramer. Kramer's death had changed a lot of things.

Larson was ready to mount when I reined up beside him. He said, his tone neutral, "Howdy, Ed."

"Howdy," I said. "I figured you boys might be gone before I got here."

"We've been hanging around," he said glumly, "but we decided we'd better slope out of here before Kramer gets back. He fired all of us this morning, but we haven't been in any hurry to pull out. We've worked here too long. It's been home. We hate like hell to leave. No job. No nothing, and winter coming on. Reckon we'll be riding the grub line."

They were all watching me. I guess they were wondering why I'd come back and if I had anything to say that would affect them. I said, "Don't ride out till I've had a chance to talk to Mrs. Kramer. He's dead. Her sister blew the top of his head off with a shotgun a little while ago."

I heard a strange sound come out of them, as if all the air in their lungs had been driven out of the chests. They couldn't think of anything to say for several seconds, then Sandy McGraw broke the silence with, "The hell! You sure?"

"I'm sure."

"But Mrs. Kramer's sister?" Larson shook his big head. "No sense in that, seems like."

"It's a long story," I said, "but she's hated him for a long time. The day she got to town on the stage she told me she'd come to kill him when the time was right. The time was right today, I guess."

I reined Alexander around and rode across the yard to the house, dismounted and tied at the hitch rail. I walked up the path to the porch and touched the brim of my hat. I said, "Howdy, Mrs. Kramer."

She barely nodded and said, "Good afternoon, Sheriff."

She seemed fatter than ever. She was fanning herself, although the afternoon had turned cold with the clouds down to the base of the mountains on both sides of the valley. Snow was falling not very far above the valley floor, but she was hot. I wondered how she could possibly run Anchor, or if she would even try.

"I have bad news, Mrs. Kramer," I said. "Your husband was shot and killed this afternoon."

It didn't shock her. She sat looking across the valley at the ranches on the west side of the river. She didn't look at me; her expression did not change when she asked, "Who did it?"

"Your sister Caroline."

I thought this would jar her all the way down to her heels, but it didn't. Her expression didn't change. She said a surprising thing, "It isn't bad news, Sheriff. It's the best news I've heard for a long time. I'm not surprised Caroline did it. She's hated him a long time. She wanted him when he first came to work for us. Finally she seduced him, then claimed he raped her. He didn't, of course. He still didn't want to have anything to do with her. It was natural that she'd hate him enough to kill him. You've heard how it is with a woman scorned. She keeps saying Dan would eventually kill me and he would have, but that wasn't the reason she killed him."

She turned her head slowly as if it was an effort, then said, her gaze meeting mine, "Yes, I'm sure he would have killed me sooner or later if I hadn't died a natural death or left him, and I would never have done that, not unless he turned over his money to me, which really was mine in the first place. He wouldn't ever have done that."

She was silent a moment, frowning thoughtfully. Then she went on, "He had big dreams about the future, you know, and I wasn't in them. I guess you're surprised that I'm telling you all of this now that he's dead, but I'm quite sure Caroline has told you her side and it wouldn't be exactly what I've just told you. Is that right?"

I was too astonished by the way she was pouring out her feelings to say anything for a few seconds. Then I nodded. "Yes, her story was a little different."

"It would be," she said. "Caroline has always been a person to take charge. I suppose she thinks she'll come out here and live with me and run Anchor." She shook her head. "Well she won't. For the first time in my life I'm going to run my own affairs. Dan married me for the ranch, you know. Then Dan ran everything. He never listened to me. Fact is, he never listened to anyone once he'd made up his mind about something."

I stood on the ground below the porch looking up at this woman who hardly seemed aware of my presence. She was talking because she had to talk to someone and I was the handy one. It seemed odd that she didn't ask how it happened. She seemed satisfied and relieved simply to know that Kramer was dead.

"Dan abused me, you know," she went on in a toneless voice. "I think I would have killed him myself if we had lived together much longer. I didn't know that Caroline was here, but I'm not surprised. She was never one to forgive a slight." She paused, frowning, and then she raised a hand and made a languid motion toward the valley. "I love this country. It's a beautiful place to spend the rest of my life. As soon as we got here, I asked Dan to give up the deal he was working on and to settle down here and raise cattle. He laughed at me."

"What was this deal he was so anxious to make?" I asked.

Her frown deepened, her gaze returning to my face. "You knew about it?"

"I knew he had a deal going," I said, "but I've never heard what it was."

"The last time he went to Denver for a stockmen's convention," she said, "he met an English lord. I don't remember his name. All I know about him is that he's rich. He and some other English nobleman were looking for a cattle ranch that was self-supporting and big enough to give them room to hunt and fish.

"It had to be a big valley or basin so he and his blue blood friends could own it all, or at least control it. It was to be a sort of kingdom set off by itself. Dan had never been here, but he had known Jordan for a long time and Jordan had described his outfit to him. When he saw an ad in a stockmen's journal that Anchor was for sale, he knew it was exactly what the Englishman wanted and he saw a fortune in it for him."

She had run out of breath. She paused, breathing so hard she was almost panting. She went on, "Dan came here, looked the place over, and made a deal with Jordan that was to be completed later when he returned. He got an agreement and a down payment from the Englishman. He was to deliver both Anchor and the land west of the river. He hired a man named Lambert to come and kill a couple of the men whose land he wanted. He said that would make all the others come to terms with him. I told him it was murder and he'd hang for it, but he laughed at me and said he aimed to be the law in Turner County."

She moved a leg as if it was an effort and scratched a thigh, then took a deep breath, her monstrous breasts rising and falling with her breathing. "But it didn't work for him did it?" she asked.

"No," I said. "It didn't work."

"I just wanted to sit here and look at the valley and the mountains," she said. "But it was a million-dollar deal and Dan had always wanted to be a millionaire. I guess the Englishman had more money than brains."

"I've got to get back to town," I said. "I thought you'd want to know about your husband."

"Thank you for riding out here to tell me," she said.

I started to turn away but then swung back as if I had just remembered something. "Mrs. Kramer, I understand that your old crew is riding in. Do you want them to work for you, or do you want to keep Jordan's men on? If my opinion is of any value to you, I'd like to say they're good men."

"These men who are riding are not my old crew," she said. "Not a one of them worked for us when Daddy was alive. Dan picked every one of them and I want no part of them. Go tell Jordan's men that I want to talk to them."

Again I turned, and as I walked away, she said, "They are bastards, all of them. I don't want them on my place."

I mounted and rode across the yard to the men who were waiting at the corral gate. I said, "She wants to talk to you. She sounds as if she wants to keep you."

Larson's grim face was lighted by a grin that stretched from one ear to the other. "Well, by God, that's the best news we ever heard."

Several of the others nodded and said it sure as hell was. I said, "Lars, that woman is going to need a lot of help."

"She'll get all we can give her," Lars said. "We don't need nobody to tell us what to do. We've been running this outfit for the last five years or more. Pappy just looked around and said we was doing fine."

"Another thing," I said. "Kramer's old crew figures they've got jobs here and they won't take his killing kindly. They may show up out here. The missus says they're bastards and she doesn't want them on the place."

"Then they won't hang around here very long," Larson said, patting the butt of his gun. "We'll give 'em a reception they won't forget. Don't worry, Ed. Everything's gonna be all right out here."

"The world's changing," I said.

"Ain't it now," Larson agreed, still grinning.

I nodded and started back to town. I had plenty of time, I thought, or I hoped I had, before Kramer's men showed up in Purgatory. I didn't know what to expect when they got there, but I had to look for the worst. From everything I'd heard about them, they were a hard-case crew who would want to square Dan Kramer's death.

A mile from the ranch the road swung close to the edge of the bench. I looked at the river and saw a line of riders moving toward town. My heart dived as I realized I was going to be too late. They were at least a mile closer to town than I was and they were moving at a fast pace.

I put Alexander into a run, knowing there was no way on this good earth I could beat them to town.

Chapter XXV

I was cold before I reached town and wished as I had a dozen times since I'd left home that I'd brought my coat. Black clouds had covered the sun and snowflakes were starting to drift earthward in their lazy, floating way when there was no wind. I had a hunch that this first storm of the fall would turn out to be a stem-winder.

When I reached the upper end of Main Street I forgot all about the snow or being cold. The men I had seen headed for town were gathered in the street in front of the hotel. Doc Wardell was standing on the boardwalk talking to them and motioning with his hands. That meant he was worked up about something.

I reined up in front of Clancy's Bar, dismounted, tied and loosened my gun in the holster. As I started walking toward the mounted men, I heard Doc shout, "Damn it, the bodies are in my back room. I tell you to come in and look at them. It's Dan Kramer and Charlie Lambert all right, but there's not much left of Kramer's face to look at."

I stayed on the boardwalk until I passed the men, then I turned and stood waiting on the outer edge of the walk. They were to all appearances just as hard-bitten a crew as I had heard. They were all young men except the one who sat his saddle a little in front of the others. He was about forty, and I guessed he was the foreman. The rest were in their early twenties, all bearded, reckless-eyed men who were plainly edgy. All were armed with rifles in their boots and Colts in holsters on their hips.

The oldest man said, "We've worked for Dan Kramer a long time, old man. We expected to work for him here. If he's dead, I guess we'll just have to ride out to the ranch he bought and work for his widow."

"I ain't sure this old man is telling the truth," one of the young ones said. "You'd best go look at those bodies, Mel."

"Why would he lie?" the older man asked.

The one who had spoken shrugged his shoulders. "I dunno, but I don't figger there's anybody in this burg who could gun Dan Kramer down. Maybe he just wants us out of town and wants us to keep riding. Maybe they don't like Dan."

"I'll go take a look," Mel said.

He followed Doc into his office. The others shifted around in their saddles, looking at me and glancing away as if trying to ignore me. I didn't know what to do, but I had a hunch something was going to explode as soon as Mel came out of Doc's office, so I figured I'd just have to wait until it did.

Mel wasn't gone long. When he staggered back into the street, he looked as if he had been stricken with a sudden, gut-wrenching sickness. He got to his horse and, grabbing the horn, stood there shivering. It wasn't, I thought, from the cold.

"Well?" one of the men asked.

"It's Dan, all right," Mel said. "What's left of him. Looking at what's left of his face is enough to give a man nightmares for a month. Most of his head's gone. They just blasted him with a God-damned scattergun."

I stepped into the street as I said, "You boys best ride back to where you came from. I just rode in from Anchor. That's the spread Kramer bought. There's nothing for you there. Mrs. Kramer is keeping the old crew that worked for Pappy Jordan."

"We ain't riding nowhere till we get the son of a bitch who blowed Dan's head off," Mel said. "Then we may just burn this town down. If you don't turn the killer over to us, we will. That's a promise."

"The law will deal with the person who killed Kramer," I said. "We wouldn't turn over a coyote to you. Now get riding and keep going till you're out of the county."

Doc was watching closely from the walk. I took another step into the street, my gaze pinned on Mel. I figured that if there was going to be any powder burned, he'd be the one to start it. He looked at me, his lips curling in distaste.

"You're too much of a kid to be wearing that star," he said. "Just who the hell are you?"

"I'm the sheriff of Turner County," I said. "Now get out of town or I'll jail the lot of you."

"Oh no, you'll never jail us, boy," Mel said and stepped away from his horse.

The thought flashed through my mind that this was the windup, that after going through all I had since I'd pinned on the star, I was going to be smoked down on Purgatory's Main Street by six men I had never seen before, men I had no fight with.

I think Mel would have gone for his gun then, and if he had, the others would have, too, but before Mel could make his move, Doc called, "Don't try it, mister," and raised an arm over his head.

Within a matter of seconds every door on Main Street, except Simon Ross's bank door, slammed open and people erupted through them. All of them carried a gun of some sort. Mark Vance had a Winchester, Beulah Heston had her revolver, Caroline Dallas had her shotgun, the bartenders in the saloons had shotguns, and even Caleb, running along the street from the parsonage, was carrying a Winchester. Hubey was there, too, with his scattergun. There were fifteen or more people lined along the boardwalks, their guns covering the men in the street. To me the most surprising was Dave Farris. He hadn't gone home as I had expected; the courage he had finally found had not leaked out of him.

"I guess if you want to make your play," I told Mel, "go ahead, but it's the last you'll ever make. I know these people. They'll blow you out of your saddles."

"That's right," Doc said.

They looked along both sides of the street, the five on their horses, Mel on the ground, and I could see them begin to wilt like tender plants that had been hit by the first fall frost. "Drop your gunbelts to the ground," I ordered. "I'm not letting you leave here and turn around and come back and kick up more trouble."

They stared at me as if I had asked them to climb to the moon. One of them gasped, "You want our guns?"

"You're damned right I do," I said. "Pronto."

They hesitated, then Mel loosened his gun belt and tossed it toward the boardwalk. Slowly the rest followed. I said, "Now your Winchesters."

"We'll get you for this," one of them fumed. "By God, we'll come back and —"

"I don't think so, Joey," Mel said. "All I want to do is to get out of this loco town."

The Winchesters were jerked from boots and dropped to the ground, then Mel mounted and without a glance at any of us, cracked steel to his horse and led the crew out of town, across the bridge that spanned the North Fork, and disappeared toward Gunnison.

We stood frozen until we could not hear or see them, then someone laughed, a high, quivering titter that seemed to release our tension. I pulled my bandanna from my pocket and wiped my face, and before I could say or do anything else, everyone crowded around me. Beulah and Caroline included, and shook my hand and said warmly they were proud of me and were glad I was the sheriff.

I shook their hands, dazed and not thinking very straight. One moment I had been figuring on seeing Saint Peter and suddenly the tables were turned and my self-appointed deputies had saved my life and probably the town.

All of a sudden I felt like crying, a good feeling, a crying in relief, I guess, because I knew now beyond any doubt that I had grown up. I had proved myself to everyone except Simon Ross, who was probably watching the whole scene from the safety of his bank. In the last few days since Judge Willoughby had asked me to serve as sheriff I had gone down into the valley and had come out of the other side to where the sun was shining, the clouds and snow notwithstanding.

"I thank all of you," I finally managed to say. "I didn't expect this kind of backing. You must have done some organizing."

Doc grinned. "As a matter of fact, we did. After the way you've held up the last two, three days, it only seemed fair that we do a little bit to help ourselves."

I saw Caroline Dallas watching me, smiling a little, and I thought there were some things I'd never know, such as whether Kramer had raped her or she had seduced him. Then I looked at Beulah who was grinning all over her fat face and I told myself I'd never know whether she slept with all the drummers who came to town or not. I looked at Caleb who was a very happy man and I thought it didn't make much difference who won the argument with Doc Wardell about whether a man who committed suicide was saved or not.

I could go on down the line. We all had our problems. We all had done things we weren't proud of and didn't want anyone else to know, but the important part of this whole business was that we had survived, all but Gramp Campbell. I wasn't sure about Pa, but I had every reason to hope that he would make it.

Then I glanced back of Beulah and saw Sharon standing there, watching and smiling and waiting. I held out my arms to her and she ran into them. I kissed her right there in front of most of Purgatory. They cheered, and someone yelled, "When are you going to tie the knot?"

Sharon drew back, whispering, "Whenever your father can come to the wedding."

"Soon," I yelled. "You hear, Caleb? Soon." The snow had piled up until it covered the ground and was coming down so hard that we couldn't see to the other end of the street, and no one seemed to notice.

We hope you have enjoyed this Large Print book. Other Thorndike, Wheeler or Chivers Press Large Print books are available at your library or directly from the publishers.

For more information about current and up-coming titles, please call or write, without obligation, to:

Publisher
Thorndike Press
295 Kennedy Memorial Drive
Waterville, ME   04901
Tel. (800) 223-1244

Or visit our Web site at:
www.gale.com/thorndike
www.gale.com/wheeler

OR

Chivers Large Print
published by BBC Audiobooks Ltd
St James House, The Square
Lower Bristol Road
Bath BA2 3BH
England
Tel. +44(0) 800 136919
email: bbcaudiobooks@bbc.co.uk
www.bbcaudiobooks.co.uk

All our Large Print titles are designed for easy reading, and all our books are made to last.